NOT BY ↳

Only the Royal Navy and a few miles of sea stand between Britain and Napoleon's Armée d'Angleterre

Paul Weston

www.paulwestonauthor.com

For Martin and Cicely

Contents

BOOK 1 – A BRITTLE PEACE

Morlaix had fought in America for the *ancien régime* against the English, the *ci-devants* believing that aiding the Americans would benefit them, not realising until too late that the germ of revolution is contagious. That germ had infected Morlaix, and when he returned home to Rosko, he became an active participant in the turbulence sweeping Brittany and all of France. When the King called the States General in 1789, he became a deputy of the Third Estate, and went to Versailles.

At Versailles, he had been shocked at its opulence and dismayed by the contempt shown towards the deputies by some of the aristos of the Second Estate. It had been natural for the Bretons to stick together, and they had formed an association, the Club Breton. When they were moved to Paris, at what with hindsight was the start of the Revolution, they set up the club in the Jacobin monastery on Rue St Honoré. Members from outside Brittany joined, and before long the Club Breton became the Jacobin Society.

Not many of the founder members of the Jacobins were left, but Morlaix had known all the great men – Mirabeau, Danton, Robespierre, Marat. He had met Odile, his wife, in Paris, a woman of the south and a fervent revolutionary who had hauled on the traces of a gun carriage during the October March to Versailles.

He had sat "on the mountain", and perhaps, he thought, his hands were not as clean as they should have been, but he had survived the Terror, in part because he was often away, fighting the enemies of the Republic, mostly the English. He had been at Toulon when the fleet was burned, and that is where he had met Napoléon Bonaparte for the first time.

In Paris he had assisted Murat when he brought up the guns for Bonaparte's "whiff of grapeshot", saving the Revolution. He had helped to bring Bonaparte back from Egypt, and had been at his side on 18 Brumaire when Napoléon had dismissed the Directory.

He realised that Bonaparte was a truly great man, possessed of some irresistible quality which marked him out. Morlaix knew and liked Talleyrand, and thought him a great man in a way, in equal measures admired and despised, but he did not have Napoléon's gift. Bonaparte could work his magic on all ranks. Left among common soldiers, he would show a genuine interest in their backgrounds, their work and even their weapons, and before long they would love and unhesitatingly obey him. He abandoned his army in Egypt, after an adventure of breathtaking folly and brutality, but he was not blamed, but rather on his return he was acclaimed and took over the Republic. His enemies feared him, and on the battlefield his presence alone was worth several regiments.

Morlaix denied, even to himself, that he had allied himself to Napoléon through self-interest, but he knew that it had not harmed his prospects. He had a generous pension, a wonderful house, and a wife who was perhaps the best connected person in Paris, with everyone who mattered striving for admittance to her salon.

Bonaparte called him "my Captain" or sometimes "my Breton".

"My Breton will arrange it" was an expression Napoléon frequently used when Morlaix was in his presence. Morlaix knew exactly what he was doing, using flattery to get his way, but nevertheless he could not help himself responding in the way Bonaparte expected. Nobody could help themselves.

Morlaix felt as if he had been rebelling, intriguing, fighting, adventuring and politicking all his adult life. He knew he'd been lucky, very lucky to have survived and even to have prospered. The raid on Weymouth was something he had been planning for years, and now that it was over, with no return on the time, money and lives expended, he felt tired, tired beyond measure, exhausted and ready to retire to Brittany, or even to America, and to enjoy a quiet life. France and the Republic had had their portion of Morlaix.

The summons to the Tuileries Palace came one morning. In the room with the First Consul were Murat, in a splendid uniform of his own design, and Talleyrand, equally well dressed but not ostentatiously so.

"My Breton," said Bonaparte in greeting, and Morlaix knew he was lost.

"We know that France is surrounded by enemies. The European ones can be dealt with, but England is the problem. The Republic will never prosper and be safe with England unconquered. I myself was thwarted, robbed of my destiny by them at Acre."

He struck the table in front of him with the flat of his hand.

From the corner of his eye, Morlaix saw Talleyrand raise a despairing hand to his brow, and he knew why – both of them agreed that Bonaparte habitually confused his destiny with that of the Republic.

"England must be subdued. I can do it in two weeks if my army is there."

Here it comes, Morlaix thought, resisting the urge to relate the joke made by the English Admiral Jervis: "*I do not say that the French cannot come, only that they cannot come by sea.*"

Instead, he said, "The boats at Boulogne? The army there?"

Napoléon held up his hand. "You know the problem with Boulogne, Breton. The cardinal."

He nodded towards Talleyrand. It always amused Morlaix when he was reminded that Talleyrand, that cynical, devious and even perhaps corrupt man, was nominally a churchman.

"… and I have just returned from that place, and you know what the English are like. If there's a foot of water, their Navy will be there. Everything at Boulogne is in plain sight from their ships cruising just offshore. They harass us, and even make raids. We have beaten them off, but they frustrate progress, and as soon as we launch our boats, their fleet will be upon us."

The First Consul leaned forward. "Murat has a plan, but, Breton, I need you to execute it."

Despite his ridiculous dress, Morlaix knew Murat to be a very capable man, clever and ruthless. He had seen Murat in action and knew that he should never be underestimated. If Murat had a plan, it was worth considering.

"Morlaix, there is another way …."

----------✳✳----------

The soiree was to be a brilliant affair, like all the soirees organised by Odile at their house, with *ton* in attendance. Morlaix could not say that he enjoyed them much, but Odile insisted that they were necessary to maintain their position, and they certainly pleased their daughter, Dominique.

Before the guests arrived, Morlaix had taken Odile and Dominique to the library. As they sat round a small table, he felt immensely proud of his wife and daughter, alike striking, beautiful and capable.

"The First Consul has given me a task."

They both looked at him, horrified. It was his habit not to tell them much about his work, but when the raid on Weymouth had become famous, he had told them of his actions, and no doubt they had heard other accounts, probably unreliable and exaggerated. He was sure that they were proud of his contribution to the Republic, but they were apprehensive for his safety. He tried to reassure them.

"It is primarily an administrative position, but of great importance, in Brittany. I will have to move there."

Odile was a loyal wife, and he had no doubt that if he had asked, she would have gone with him, but she was enmeshed in politics in Paris.

"Who will look after your interests here if you are in Brittany? God knows you have enemies."

Morlaix had not really thought of that, and admitted as such.

"I think I should stay here, at least for a while …."

"Is it a very great task, Father?" interrupted Dominique. "If so, it is my duty to go with you."

She fingered the tricolour sash she wore. Morlaix thought that she had not had his experience, and had therefore not acquired his own deep cynicism. He hoped she never would.

"I will certainly go with you to Brittany." She looked at Odile.

"You cannot go to Brittany, Dominique. The Chouans, the filthy Royalists, the *ci-devants*." Odile looked at her husband. "What would happen if they got hold of her?"

"Our First Consul has pretty well stopped all that. It would be a brave Chouan who tried anything now."

He knew by the look in Dominique's eyes that there would be no stopping her.

----------✳✳✳----------

The soiree glittered, perhaps on this occasion even more than usual. Their guests included Talleyrand and, to his horror, Fouché, recently replaced by Napoléon as minister of police, but still with a wide network of spies and informers and as wicked as ever. The Peace of Amiens had allowed the English to travel to Paris, and there were several in attendance. Mostly they were substantial men, chosen for their influence by either their Embassy or Talleyrand, but he noticed a pair of young men who, despite their stylish dress, seemed to him to have the air of the quarterdeck about them – naval men. One of them even seemed familiar.

He made little effort to engage with the English guests, feeling that they might not be well disposed towards him, even if they were in his house drinking his wine.

Talleyrand and some of his acquaintances were sat around a card table, and Morlaix watched as one of the two young Englishmen joined them. God help him, he thought, he'll have an entertaining but expensive time. Odile introduced Morlaix to two women who were eager to hear of his recent activities, and he was distracted.

When he looked around again, he saw that Dominique was animatedly talking to the younger of the English officers, a fine-looking young man, the one that seemed familiar. The contrast between her happiness and optimism and Morlaix's world of war, revolution, great plans and politics made him feel suddenly exhausted, and he went upstairs to bed.

Chapter 2 – Paid Off

The frigate was badly knocked about, and it was obvious that she was going to require considerable work before she was fit for sea again. That she would be required at sea one day was also obvious. Nobody seemed to expect the Peace of Amiens to last long, and when it ended, every ship would be needed to blockade the French and stop them crossing the Channel for their long-cherished project of the invasion of England. I was pretty well recovered from my ordeal and determined to get back home to Portland as soon as I could. Snowden, my shipmate and now fellow midshipman, was also keen to leave the ship, but apparently less keen to go to his home.

"Jack, I've been in ships, one way or another, since I was twelve. I haven't been home all that much, and when I do it's pretty dispiriting. I may be a lordling, but certainly not a gilded one. Father drinks, mother has what might be called an "active social life", and the place in Cornwall is falling down. There's no money at all."

It took me a bit of time to register that Snowden might be some sort of aristocrat, though I had heard the odd sarcastic remark addressed to "your lordship".

"What do you mean, 'lordling'?"

"I'm in line to become Lord Penzance, for what it's worth, when my father shuffles off"

"What is it worth?"

"A dreary and damp family pile, and a pile of debts as well, but it does have its advantages. Even now, the Honourable Percy Snowden, me, is able to get away with things that you commoners can only dream about. Sounds like we're both headed west. Shall we string along together?"

It seemed as though I could hardly refuse, and we walked to the Town Quay and, after negotiation, hired a boat to take us to Lymington.

"We can get a coach there," said Snowden.

We set off, the boat with the tide under her making good progress along the Solent, as we sat on our sea chest. There was enough spray to make us glad of our boat cloaks, but the evening was warm and clear when we went alongside at Lymington. The quay was bustling as we paid off the boatman and made our way through the crowd to the inn. When I say "we" paid off the boatman, I really meant that I paid him off, using a few of the large store of coins I'd been given at the celebratory dinner in Portsmouth.

At the inn, we took a room and went down to dinner. We were served by a pretty girl, Carrie, who Snowden seemed to get along with very well. That was Snowden; he had the gift of getting along with almost anyone, particularly women, and his easy manner and assurance seemed to let him fit into any social situation. After dinner, as we sat in the public room, we were invited to play at cards with some locals. I declined, but Snowden joined them and before long was the heart of the gathering, although by the time I went upstairs there seemed to be some at the table who regretted his invitation.

I awoke as the sun shone through the window. Snowden was still deeply asleep, and I had a dim memory of him returning very late. I went down into the public room and sat at a table, where I was joined after half an hour or so by Snowden.

"Snowden, how are you?"

"Very well, very well indeed."

He patted his pocket, in a gesture I was destined to know so well, and said quietly. "Successful night, Jack. All that time at sea – it seems that practice does make perfect."

Carrie came into the room, and Snowden turned towards her. "Carrie, how about some food?"

We ate our breakfast, with Snowden and Carrie keeping up a lively conversation. Afterwards, we walked along the town quay, which was crowded with shipping. A fishing boat, about twenty-five feet long, was dried out in the little dock there, with an elderly man working on her. Her name, *Jill*, was highlighted in white letters on her black transom. Snowden, in his easy way, was soon on the beach talking to the fisherman, and it transpired that the man was giving up the sea and was intending to sell the boat.

"Son's away to sea, volunteered for the Navy. Bosun now and doing well, with a bit of prize money. No interest in taking it up."

The sight of the boat, so reminiscent of the *Jean Renee* I had stolen to make my escape from France in, brought back memories, and I sighed.

"What's up, Jack?" said Snowden.

"I know we have to fight the French, but I'm not sure I'm cut out for it. It's easier when I was on the frigate, and there were people all around, telling me what to do, but being on my own in France was very trying. You know I killed a man, deliberately, hand to hand. He was a bad man, it was him or me, and I had to do it, but I heard him scream as he fell over the cliff. I felt sorry for him, and I still think of it, frequently, even dream about it sometimes."

Sometimes – every night in reality. Snowden put his hand on my shoulder.

"And what is the point of it, that's what I don't understand? Why can't the French leave us alone? I stole that French family's boat, just like this one. What are they to do without it?"

We went back to the inn and sat in the bow window of the public room, looking out on the busy quay.

Carrie put glasses of Madeira in front of us. Snowden drank, and pulled a face.

"Disgusting stuff. Perhaps we'll be able to get some decent claret again now the war's over. Cheer up Jack, at least you've got a welcoming home to go to, and a pension from the King."

The thought that a peer, or at least a future peer, would be envious of me, the son of a Portland smuggler, seemed ridiculous.

"But you've got a huge house and will be a lord. With your connections you'll get promoted quickly in the Navy."

He laughed. "No, Jack, it doesn't work like that. My father managed to get me taken on as captain's servant to my uncle when I was twelve, really because he couldn't afford to educate me. But that's as far as it goes. My uncle, who might be able to do something for me, has sons of his own, and he doesn't really approve of his brother."

He leaned forward. "Look, Jack, I've had an idea. Probably ridiculous, but there we are. The people who I was playing with last night," he tapped his pocket, which jingled pleasantly, "were saying that everybody who can is off to France now. Look at this."

He took up the copy of *The Times*, a few days old, which he'd been reading at breakfast, found the place, and showed it to me.

"It says here that Paris is full of English, and the French are even putting on a special exhibition for us at the Louvre. Why don't we," he stopped, "I mean you, buy that boat, and we can take it to France and give it to your distressed fisherman?"

I sat back, amazed, but we were both young and foolish and I didn't stop him; in fact I felt a surge of excitement and gulped down my glass.

"You're pretty well minted now. I will have my pay, and," he patted his jingling pocket again, "I expect I can top up as we go along. Paris, man, it'll be like paradise."

I was thinking more of the boat and the voyage than the remotely imagined joys of Paris, but, well, I'd had the Madeira, and when we walked back to the dock, the tide was nearly full and *Jill* was floating, very pretty, and an hour later she was mine.

We spent the next few days in Lymington. The fisherman, Mr Cowman, was very good to us, although he clearly had mixed feelings about the departure of his boat. He took us downriver, into the Solent, and "showed us the ropes". *Jill* was well equipped, and sailed well with her lug sail. We had no trouble at all in handling her. Our stay at the inn was pleasant, although there was a distinct lack of volunteers to play at cards with Snowden after the first night.

"I think it's time to go, Jack. Wind'll be north-west tomorrow, top of the tide ten o'clock."

At our departure at eight there was a distinct contrast between the attitude of Mr Cowman, who wished us well, and Carrie, who was frosty and who ended every sentence she addressed to Snowden with a "my lord" in a far from affectionate tone.

We sailed down the Lymington River and into the choppy Solent, the boat going well, and then a fine tramp past Hengistbury Head. We passed the entrance to Poole Harbour, anchoring for the night off Studland. *Jill*'s draft was quite deep, and as we had no boat, we couldn't get ashore, much to Snowden's chagrin, as we could see the lights of an inn just up from the beach.

At first light we were underway, passing well offshore of the Kimmeridge Ledges, before the wind went round to the south-west and things became rather uncomfortable. Portland was directly to windward, so we decided to go into Weymouth, arriving about seven. It seemed a long time since I'd been there.

The quay was bustling, and we went into the Ship Inn. I hadn't realised that in my absence I had become famous, at least locally, and there was quite a crowd around us as we ate, and the landlord would take no money. Snowden was very much in his element, and the tale of the chase across the Channel and the battle at the Nez de Jobourg lost nothing in the telling. Before long, he was ensconced in a card game, assisted by a rather good-looking girl leaning over his shoulder. I hoped he wasn't too distracted. I was glad to hear from the landlord that *Cicely*'s crew were free from captivity in France and were thought to be on their way home

Snowden came into the bedroom very late again, and was still asleep when I got up early and went to check *Jill* alongside the quay, tugging gently at her lines in the brisk south-westerly. I wasted quite a bit of time looking at her from different angles, admiring her lines and freshly blacked sides, not quite used to the pride of ownership.

I walked around the town and into Piplers, the chandlers, more for interest's sake than to search for a particular item. There was a section devoted to charts and books. Until then, I hadn't really given much thought about the actual business of navigating to France, but I realised when I looked at the charts of the French coast that this was something I could not take for granted. The previous Jack Stone method of "heading north (or south as the case may be) and hoping for the best" was not something I cared to repeat. As well as the charts, there was a large book, even more fascinating, called *Le Petit Neptune Français*, which I had not heard of before. The frontispiece showed a view of the famous Cardouan lighthouse at the mouth of the Gironde, and the text, accompanied by small charts and illustrations, was a comprehensive guide to the coast of France. As usual on these occasions, I wrestled with the prospect of the expenditure involved, but in the end bought not only the charts and the *Petit Neptune* but also a pair of dividers, and a steering compass as well.

Back at the Ship, before sitting down to breakfast, I looked at the schedule on the wall for the fly to Dorchester, where I knew Snowden could take a coach to Cornwall, assuming that he would want to visit his people before we set off for France. I sat down at a table and was engrossed in the *Petit Neptune*, specifically the section on the Race of Alderney, which read "*The tides are extremely strong in this passage ... the swiftness of this current in spring tides is about two leagues per hour*", when Snowden sat down beside me.

"How'd you do, Jack?"

I looked at him. "Another late night?"

For a moment he looked sheepish, just for a moment. "What's that you've got there?"

I showed him the book.

"*Petit Neptune.* Damn, that's worth having." He grabbed it and riffled through the pages. "Look, here's the bit about the Basque Roads."

Our food arrived, and when we'd finished I said, "The fly goes to Dorchester at ten. You can get the coach from there."

He looked at me. "Jack, I've been meaning to speak to you about this. I was wondering if perhaps we could set off for France quite soon. The weather's likely to be better earlier in the year, and, well, I don't really relish the prospect of going home. I feel Paris is calling me." For once, Snowden looked embarrassed. "I thought perhaps we could take *Jill* to Portland. I could stay somewhere near your house, and we could get the boat ready and set off as soon as the weather serves."

The Honourable Percy Snowden wanted to stay on Portland! I began to realise just how grim the family seat must be.

"Perce, I don't really know what to say. You'd be welcome, of course, but it is not what you're used to and …"

"Yes?"

"Well, Portland's pretty isolated, wild even. The people are quite poor, and if you go gambling with them and take what little money they have, they won't take kindly to it. I don't know what will happen, but it won't end well for anyone probably."

I took a breath and went on. "The other thing, the women might be, there's a lot of widows, and wives with husbands away to sea, I don't really know what to say, but …"

I tailed off.

"I think I know what you mean, Jack – 'Snowden, behave'."

"That's about the size of it."

"Don't worry, I'll be good as gold."

And he was.

We set off about noon, against a brisk south-westerly, and as we drew nearer to Portland, I could see a small knot of people on the beach. With a start I realised that my parents were among them. Word must have spread that I was in Weymouth, about to return. As *Jill*'s forefoot grated on the shingle I jumped overboard, heedless of the waist-deep water, and ran up the beach to embrace them.

We spent the days preparing the boat for the journey, and the evenings looking at charts and the *Petit Neptune*, and relating our adventures to various audiences. Snowden's stock of anecdotes was by no means small. He had had an adventurous time in the Navy and was widely travelled, but he always listened attentively to the anecdotes of other people.

My parents were bemused by the way that events had unfolded, and were not altogether enthusiastic about our proposed voyage to France. Our determination was obvious though, and they were reassured by Snowden's participation.

At last we were ready, the courses plotted, the boat provisioned. All we needed was a bit of good weather, but to our frustration the wind remained obdurately in the south.

We were standing on the ridge of the Chesil beach one evening, with the sun setting in a lurid red sky. The wind, obstinately in the south, dropped completely, and then returned almost immediately as a fine breeze from the north-east.

Snowden recited:
> *"Fair stood the wind for France*
> *When we our sails advance,*
> *Nor now to prove our chance*
> *Longer will tarry ...."*

I took the hint and we ran back to the cottage, collected our gear and my parents, and they rowed us out to *Jill*, anchored just offshore. There were no tears or untoward demonstration of emotions. I think my father was confident of our abilities, and my mother's more or less complete belief in the abilities of my father was rapidly being transferred to me.

We hoisted the main and mizzen, and sailed the anchor out. We slid along the black bulk of the Isle, high and forbidding in silhouette against the fading light. I kept close inshore, to take advantage of the eddy there, and we were soon bouncing in the disturbed water near the Bill. Before long we were out of sight of the lighthouses, and it was dark until the moon rose. Occasionally we struck a light to look at the compass, but as we took our tricks at the helm, we selected a star in the bright heavens to steer by.

We made good progress, the man off watch lying on the bottom boards, ready to assist if necessary, and the boat running well, with the wake hissing behind us and the occasional roar of the bow wave as she slid down a roller. It was cold but the boat was perfectly dry inside. We saw the dancing lights of ships and boats, mostly passing up and down the Channel, but none came close to us. I knew the wind was getting up, and when the dawn came it was clear that we were overcanvassed, so we pulled down a reef in the mainsail. By ten o'clock we could make out the Caskets, and then Alderney in the distance, and by noon were close enough to the Caskets to make out the details of the lighthouse, with Guernsey plainly visible ahead. The sea was dotted with sails, merchant ships, men o' war, and fishermen.

We recorded our progress on the chart, and, assiduously following the directions in the *Petit Neptune*, were soon in the Little Russell between Guernsey and Herm, the wind now quite light and the tide fair. Rocks were everywhere, but we followed the leading marks, and before long entered St Peter's. By five in the evening we were safely alongside the quay, and soon afterwards the harbourmaster came aboard.

An hour or so later we were sitting in the boat when a distinguished-looking gentleman approached.

"Good evening," he said. "The harbourmaster has informed me that you intend to sail this vessel to France."

He looked at my companion. "It's Snowden, isn't it? You were in the cabin of *Repulse* when I visited your uncle at Gibraltar. I was with him in the old *Levant.* You've grown up since then. Mind if I …?" Indicating the boat's deck, he stepped aboard and looked round.

"How is he? Promotion a bit slow coming, I hear?"

He held out his hand and Snowden shook it.

"I don't know, sir, I haven't heard for some time."

He turned to me and offered his hand, which I took. "And you must be the famous Stone. I'm Sausmarez, James Sausmarez Captain RN." He swept his arm, indicating the island and the Russell. "This is my manor, the Channel Islands station."

I gulped. "Pleased to meet you, sir."

"And me you. You certainly put one over on the French. Now I understand you're one of us, Midshipman, and are you really taking this fine vessel to France?"

"Yes, sir."

"Good for you. Well, you must come up to the house to dinner, I expect you've some rare stories to tell, and stay as long as you like. I'll send someone down to collect you. Later."

He walked briskly off.

"That's the legendary Sausmarez," Snowden said when he'd gone.

"Why's he legendary?"

"He's done everything – Saintes, St Vincent, Nile, all of them. French tried to ambush him, but he led them a merry dance through the rocks off Guernsey, and that meant they couldn't safely cross the Channel and invade us. Did some good work last year in Algeciras. Bath and a pension I believe."

"Bath?"

"Order of the Bath. Means he's a baronet, Sir James now. Rich wife as well I've heard."

He paused and leaned forward. "Doesn't get along with Nelson."

Shortly afterwards, we were collected from the quay by a carriage with a liveried driver and footman, and taken to Sausmarez's impressive house, a short drive away from St Peter's.

Another uniformed servant met us in the hall and showed us to rooms upstairs, telling us that dinner would be at eight. As soon as the servant had gone, I knocked on Snowden's door.

"Perce, what should I do, what should I wear? What shall I say at dinner?"

"Don't worry, Jack, it'll be fine. Anyway, Sausmarez has heard about you, and I'm sure he'll make allowances for your lowly origins. Try and avoid eating with your fingers, though, it just ain't done at a baronet's table."

I laughed.

"Just wear the best clothes you have, and lay off the claret (he can't be just off the coast of France and not have claret, can he?). Now, leave me to preen. Meet me here when you hear the gong."

I went back to my room, and to my astonishment my clothes had been taken out of my chest and the most presentable of them laid on the bed. Even more astonishingly, a bath had appeared before the fire and a woman was pouring hot water into it.

When the woman had gone, I got into the bath. It was extremely pleasant, such a contrast to the windy trip across the Channel, and I started to think about the voyage and, I must admit, how well we had done. Pride cometh before a fall, and I was awakened by a hammering on the door.

"Jack, what are you doing? Are you ready? The gong was ten minutes ago."

I leapt out of the bath, feeling at first confused, and then tremendously revived after my sleep, dried myself as well as I could and dressed quickly. Snowden came into the room, laughing.

"Sorry," I said, "fell asleep in the bath."

"You're an idiot and no mistake, Stone. Invited to dinner by a baronet, and you are so excited you fall asleep."

He looked at me quizzically. "You'll do, let's go …."

----------✳✳✳----------

The dinner was an interesting experience for me. Sausmarez was a good host, and Snowden and I, especially Snowden, were captivated by his four lively daughters. Sausmarez was very interested in my story, and I gradually lost my nervousness when talking to him. I made sure that I didn't drink much of the wine, which Snowden afterwards pronounced to be "excellent".

As we drank port after dinner, Sausmarez leaned towards us over the table. "That Morlaix – he's a dangerous man. Would you believe that he went after the King? Would have got him too, if it wasn't for you, Jack. The war is coming back, I'm sure, with Boney in charge, and they can't get anywhere unless they do for us first. Once they land in England, we'll be in serious trouble."

"But they've got to get across the Channel, and surely we'll be able to stop them, sir?" said Snowden.

"They only need a few hours, couple of days at the most. All it needs is for the Navy to be distracted, or even defeated locally, and they'll take the chance. We had them bottled up before, but they nearly got over. I managed to get my ships away, through the rocks, you understand, but it could easily have gone the other way."

"Your friend Morlaix can do it if anyone can, Jack. He's Boney's right-hand man when it comes to naval matters, and between them they make a dangerous pair. Morlaix will be involved in any enterprise against us, depend on it."

----------✳✳---------

The next day Sausmarez took us round his island. I had never ridden a horse before, but my docile mount and I got on tolerably well together, and we had a very interesting day. Guernsey was not quite English, and not French either. The people spoke a language that seemed to be halfway between the two. Sausmarez was clearly well liked, and he conversed readily with the inhabitants we met.

The dinner that night was very enjoyable, with Sausmarez relating episodes of his spectacular naval career. Snowden asked him about Nelson.

"Known him a long time. I have to say, I don't really take to him, but many do. The main thing is the man seems to have no fear, of the French or anybody. I'll tell you someone else I know. Whitworth, now our man in Paris …"

"Whitworth?" asked Snowden. "Is that the man from Russia? I think he's got some family connection with us, my mother is always speaking of him."

"There you are then. I'll give you a letter of introduction, and combined with your family connection you'll be a made man when you get to Paris."

"The connection hasn't helped me much so far, but thank you very much, sir," said Snowden.

Sausmarez nodded in my direction. "Mind you don't lead that young man too seriously astray. I think the Navy can make good use of him, so don't you corrupt him to the point of uselessness."

"I'll try not to, sir," said Snowden, with a grin.

----------***---------

As the evening wore on, we discussed the route to France from Guernsey with the aid of charts and the *Petit Neptune*. Sausmarez told us about the number of English people flocking to Paris.

"Every man and his dog is there now. Some pretty disreputable types as well. You won't fit in at all," he said, looking at Snowden.

In the morning, the wind was from the south-west, favourable for us. We breakfasted in the dawn, with the Sausmarez family, who all came to St Peter's to see us off. Before we left, Sausmarez handed the letter of introduction to Snowden.

We had a fine sail that morning. Snowden was much taken by seeing the Passage Percée between Herm and Jethou on the chart, and we took that, though it made for rather anxious pilotage. Once through, we turned *Jill*'s head to the east, and before long we could see the French coast ahead of us. We were able to identify Cap de Flamanville without difficulty, and came into Dielette at about one in the afternoon.

I had put tremendous effort into getting this far, and I should have felt some elation. Snowden certainly seemed to, but the sight of what I thought to be an exceptionally dismal-looking place, one where I had spent so many hours in fear and isolation, depressed my spirits markedly.

There was a quite a large crowd on the wall, presumably waiting for the coasting ketch which we could see just offshore, making its way into the harbour. We went alongside the quay, amongst the other fishing boats, and most of the crowd gathered above us. I may have put effort into getting the boat there, but I had given almost no thought to what we would do once we got there, apart from a general idea that I would walk up to the farm and tell the family that the boat was theirs, but the crowd on the quay and their interest in us clearly made this impossible.

Snowden, speaking French, which was generally understood there, managed to convey what we were about, and there was a commotion amongst the crowd, and a couple of people detached themselves, and ran along the harbour wall towards the town.

The ketch came alongside, pretty neatly, and the process of discharging and loading cargo commenced.

"*Ou va le bateau?*" Snowden asked a woman.

"*St Malo.*"

"*La prochaine marée?*"

"*Non, directement.*"

Snowden and I waited, and before long more people arrived, one in a uniform of some kind. An elderly man spoke to Snowden, who nodded and turned towards me.

"He says they're waiting for Goulard, the man you appropriated the boat from."

I went back aboard *Jill*, and packed the charts and compass into our sea chests. Snowden walked along to the ketch, conversed with the crew, and then returned aboard.

"I've booked a passage for us on the ketch, for St Malo," he said. "I'd sooner get out of this place, I'm not at all sure about that man in uniform."

There was a stir in the crowd, and Goulard and his wife arrived. I recognised them as the people who I had seen through their window, just before I had stolen their boat.

To my surprise Goulard spoke to me in English, heavily accented, but understandable.

"You are the one who took my boat?"

"Yes."

"You are so young, you must have had terror."

"Yes, I did."

"What happened to my boat?"

"She was smashed." I gestured with both hands to indicate what had happened that night on the Kimmeridge Ledges. "I am sorry. I would like to give you this boat."

The lack of surprise showed that he had been told of my intention by the people who had gone to fetch him.

"Thank you very much. I know you English, I have been many times to Jersey and Guernsey. The war is bad."

During this exchange, Snowden was dragging the chests to the ketch with the aid of a couple of locals, and I saw them swung aboard.

"I apologise for taking your boat."

"*C'est la guerre. Merci.*"

Snowden grabbed my arm and pulled me away, towards the ketch, which had her mainsail up and scandalised, and her outer jib hoisted and flapping, men ready at the sheets.

"Let's go, Jack, the packet is a rolling."

Goulard and his wife shook my hand, looking bewildered. "*Bonne chance,*" they said almost in unison.

As we came up to the ketch, we could see her name, *Rozzen*, and her home port, Rosco, painted on her stern. As soon as our feet touched the deck they backed the outer jib until her bow pointed away from the quay, clearly anxious not to be caught by the ebbing tide. As she came round, they sheeted home the jib and let the mainsail draw. She heeled to her work, moving away from the quay.

I turned round and saw the Goulards wave at the ketch.

"*Le cidre*," he shouted, "*merci!*"

He'd obviously found the stone jar of cider which Snowden had insisted we leave on *Jill*, in return for the cider which Goulard had kept on *Jene Renee* and which I'd drunk on my voyage to England.

When *Rozzen* was a mile or so off the breakwater, she was put in irons and the enormous topsail set. She sailed close hauled in the brisk south-westerly, sometimes dipping her bowsprit and with the occasional wave running in the lee scuppers.

Snowden considered the ketch's impressive progress. "I say, she's a goer, isn't she? Real *chasse marée*."

She certainly was. I'd never seen a ship sail like her.

"Sorry to cut you short back there, but I didn't like the look of that official chap in uniform. Thought we'd take the opportunity to get out before any questions started."

"What do you mean, questions?"

"About you. Theft of a boat is a crime I expect, in France as it is in England. And you undoubtedly stole a boat, not to mention a chicken, as I remember. You're a criminal, Jack."

"But there was a war, I was doing my duty."

"Perhaps you were, but that might not be how the chap in the uniform sees things, or even people further up the chain."

"I did what I had to do."

"So you did, Jack, and England is grateful to you, but you weren't officially a combatant, and perhaps the rules of war didn't apply to you at the time. Do you know what happened to Sidney Smith and Wright?"

"I don't know anything about what happened to them, though I've heard of Smith."

"Smith is a brilliant officer. Too brilliant for some. He defended Acre in the Levant against Boney, finished off his campaign there. That was one thing, but before that he burned about half the French fleet when we withdrew from Toulon, when Boney was besieging it. He did not have a commission when he did it. Years later, the French got hold of him and his secretary, Wright – I think a cutting-out affair went wrong – and banged them up in the Temple. No exchange, just the turn of the key in the lock. They managed to escape, but the point is the French could conceivably take the same view of your activities."

I hadn't thought of that before. "What's the Temple?"

"A very nasty prison in Paris where they put the enemies of the Revolution. Look, let's get off the subject shall we?"

I looked back to where Dielette and Cap Flamanville were receding in the haze, and we went below into the ketch's rather sparse accommodation, really a cleared area of her hold.

We turned in as best we could, after bargaining for some food and cider. We were woken in the early morning by the thundering of the sails and the shift of trim as the ship was put onto the starboard tack, and we went on deck. Guernsey was visible some distance away to port, but no other land was in sight.

Bearing in mind what Snowden had said about the Temple, we kept our conversation with the ketch's crew to a minimum, as they had undoubtedly picked up some of what was going on in Dielette. Conversation with the crew was in any event difficult, as they spoke a language that I had not heard before.

"Breton," said Snowden. "Many of 'em are not particularly fond of the French anyway. Rosco, where this fine vessel hails from, is about as far away from Paris as it is possible to get."

The vessel was indeed a fine one, and with the sheets cracked off a bit she flew through the water, so that by evening we were entering St Malo, grey and impressive with its fortifications and myriad rocks. We followed the ship's progress in the *Petit Neptune*, past the fortified rocky island of Sezembre and up the channel, to lay alongside a quay in the town.

Snowden and I went ashore and hired a boy with a handcart to take our chests. St Malo was prosperous looking and orderly, and there were a number of fine-looking schooners in the harbour.

We found lodgings in the town and had a splendid meal. Snowden, as usual, was immediately at home, and before long was at a table with some quite prosperous-looking people, playing at cards.

"Probably won't be quite so prosperous when Snowden's finished with them," I said under my breath as I went up to bed.

As usual, it was very late when Snowden came up to the room and woke me.

"Jack – amazing luck tonight." He patted his breast pocket, which tinkled pleasantly. I doubted that luck had much to do with it.

"Not that lucky, Snowden, if you're sleeping up here."

"Don't be ratty, Jack, that can wait. The important thing is that I'm seriously in funds now, and we can make off to Paris tomorrow with a glad heart."

At that, he fell asleep.

In the morning, Snowden seemed very keen to be gone. I had a notion that perhaps he thought that the friends he had made last night might not be friends in the morning, after reflecting on the state of their finances.

We walked down to the docks, and found that there was a boat leaving for Dinard shortly, so we loaded our chests aboard and set off.

The journey up the river Rance was slow going. The most interesting thing we saw on the trip was what seemed to be a lock under construction in the river just before we arrived at Dinard.

"Do you think they're building a canal?" I asked Snowden.

"Wouldn't surprise me," he said. "This estuary puts you a long way inland, and it can't be all that far to the Vilaine river."

Snowden had spent quite a bit of time blockading Brittany and the west coast of France, so he had some knowledge of that region.

"I know they have a splendid canal between Toulouse and the Med – goes up hundreds of feet I believe."

The thought of going up hundreds of feet in a boat, in the middle of France, was a novel one to me.

"There's a pretty canal in England too, now. Not on the scale of the French one, but it takes coal to Manchester. It has made coal so cheap that the trades in Manchester are doing very well, I've heard. I'm pretty sure Rennes is on the Vilaine. If Froggy had the chance of getting between the Channel and Biscay without us being able to interfere, I should think he'd snap up the opportunity."

We tried to ask the boatmen about the lock, but their French was very limited, and we failed to gain any information.

We walked up the hill from the port to the town of Dinard, and put up in a coaching inn. As usual, after dinner, Snowden played at cards with some of the locals, who were perhaps not quite as prosperous-looking as those at St Malo, but still respectably dressed.

Rather than going straight upstairs, I sat in the corner and watched as the game progressed. I realised that Snowden's easy affability was a mask for intense concentration on the game, in contrast to his companions who looked about them and engaged in repartee with the woman behind the bar. Such was the intensity of Snowden's concentration that I think he would hardly have noticed if the house had caught fire.

After an hour or so, there was what was clearly a moment of some drama. The table was hushed as Snowden reached into his pocket, pulled out what seemed to be a large number of coins, and laid them on the table. The man opposite, who seemed to be the only other one in the game now, scribbled something on a scrap of paper and pushed it into the middle of the table. The excitement was so great that I stood up for a better view, and from my vantage point I could see Snowden's gold glinting expensively on the table. I watched with a feeling of dread as Snowden reached again into his pocket and added more coins to the pile. His opponent reached across the table, retrieved his scrap of paper, wrote something on it, and pushed it back into the centre. Snowden again reached for his coins, but the other player grunted.

"Non," and put his cards on the table, face up.

Snowden smiled and slowly laid his cards down. There was a collective intake of breath.

"*Merci, monsieur,*" said Snowden, as he swept the coins and the piece of paper into his pocket.

Snowden stood up and solemnly shook hands with all the players. He spoke to the man he had beaten. "*Huit heures sont pratique pour vous, monsieur, ici?*"

The man nodded.

"*Jusqu'au matin, monsieur*," said Snowden. And to me, "Jack, I think it's time we went up. I'd like to get to know the barmaid better, but I think under the circumstances I'll forgo that pleasure."

When Snowden had carefully locked the door to the room, I turned to him. "Percy, what have you done?"

"Nothing to get excited about, Jack, just a bit of good luck."

He held out the piece of paper. On it was written "*Trois bons chevaux avec des selles*", with a signature under it. I knew enough French to realise that Snowden had won three "good" horses.

"How do you do it, Percy?" I asked "Do you cheat?"

"Of course I don't cheat. That's one thing we gentlemen do not do. And remember," he paused and raised his eyebrows theatrically, "you're a gentleman now too. No, Jack, I've just got very good at playing, by practising and thinking about it. I think about it pretty well all of the time, it seems to me sometimes. There were always card games in the evening at my father's house, sometimes for pretty high stakes. My mother played, but generally lost, to the detriment of my father's fortune, and my father would have nothing to do with it. I used to watch, probably from when I was about five, and got obsessed I suppose you would say, and have been obsessed with it since. My uncle was interested in gambling. He's a very cautious man, and he did well, in a modest way. He taught me the rudiments of the system I use now."

"Blockade duty often gives considerable opportunity for playing, as undoubtedly you will come to realise if the war starts again, and I lost none of those opportunities. I have taught myself to remember all the cards that are dealt, and to study the faces and mannerisms of my opponents. I don't drink when I'm playing. It doesn't always work, but in the long run I generally come out ahead. The thing is, you have to be careful, you have to control yourself. The thing I have learned, though, is that winning doesn't always make one popular. When I realised that, after a rather unpleasant experience, I was always careful on ships to make sure that I didn't win too much or too often."

"What would have happened tonight if you'd lost?"

"Nothing much, except I would have felt my reputation damaged. I used the winnings from last night as my stake, so if I'd lost it, and I didn't gamble all of it anyway, I would have been no worse off than I was yesterday."

Chapter 9 – Brittany

The horse dealer, good as his word – "a first" said Snowden – met us at eight o'clock. He did not seem to be particularly cheerful, in contrast with Snowden's enthusiastic demeanour. We were soon in possession of three horses, in return for the scrap of paper. The horses looked splendid to me and rather large, and Snowden insisted that the journey to Paris would be much more enjoyable if we made our own way there on horseback, but I was dubious.

"We'll be able to do as we wish," Snowden said, persuasively. "The coaches in this country are foul, and the inns are not much better." He spoke with an assurance that was not justified by his possession of the facts, but I did not argue.

I had acquitted myself reasonably well riding on Guernsey, and I supposed that I would learn as we went on.

With the exchange of some coin, the saddle of one of the horses was changed for a pack harness, and we distributed the contents of our chests into its panniers. We set off as soon as we could, following the river as closely as possible. I was very curious about the canal, as it seemed a wonderful thing to me that cargoes could be transported by water so far inland.

The canal works were on a large scale, and before long we came upon another lock under construction. It seemed that the technique was to divert the river, and then to work at straightening it and levelling the bottom of it. There were hundreds of people, men and women, working, and it reminded me of the dockyard at Portsmouth, with its air of purpose and industry. The people dug, loaded carts, carried soil around, and skilled masons and other tradesmen were employed in building the locks. There was mud everywhere.

We passed several more locks, some of which were nearly finished, and stopped for a rest just beyond a village called Tinténiac. We ate our bread and cheese and drank our cider.

After a short sleep on the grass, I was woken by Snowden. "Time to move I reckon, Jack." He consulted the map and looked at the sun. "Follow the canal a bit more, I think."

A few minutes later, we pulled our horses up on a slight rise and saw what we presumed was preparation for a yard intended to build boats for the canal. An extensive area had been cleared and levelled, and buildings were being constructed. There were rows of tents for workers, and a hard surface laid along the banks of the canal. A large lake was connected to the canal by a channel.

"They must be intending to build a large number of barges," Snowden said.

"Yes," I replied, "look at those piles of timber over there."

We followed the road south for a few more miles and stopped at a house in a village, where we were able to have the horses looked after. The house had two rooms, one for animals and the other for the people, with little to choose between them for squalor. The Breton peasants wore wooden sabots on their feet, unless they were carrying them for reasons of economy. The men were dressed in canvas smocks with enormously wide trousers and wide-brimmed hats, and the women often wore elaborate bonnets. The small fields of the region were bordered by high hedges and sunken lanes, often with crude gates across them, meaning that progress away from the main roads was extremely slow and tedious.

I had done harm to the Goulard family when I had taken their boat, or rather I suppose that it was really war that had harmed them, with me as its agent. War, or at least the revolt of the Chouans, was not long over in Brittany, and it had clearly contributed to the poverty we saw around us. The local people would not discuss it with us, even when they realised we were English and not French.

By noon on the following day we were in Rennes, which was a Republican town and seemed relatively prosperous. The canal would shortly reach Rennes, and Snowden opined that the Vilaine would be canalised before long, giving a route for boats between the Channel and Biscay.

We did not hurry on our way to Paris. The journey was pleasant enough and full of interest. Life in France seemed to go on reasonably well despite the recent upheavals. Tricoleurs were often in evidence, increasingly so as we left Brittany and the bitter legacy of the Chouannerie.

Just over a week after we had set out, we stopped at Versailles, near Paris, amazed by the size and splendour of the former King's palace, damaged though it had been by the Revolution. We had seen no English people since we left St Malo, but in Versailles there was a large English presence, rather noisy.

On the following day, we entered Paris.

Snowden thought that Stone was a very pleasant chap, and frighteningly determined. He had a talent for getting things done, and though he didn't fully appreciate it yet, he had a ruthless capacity which would probably take him far.

In contrast, Snowden thought of himself as only ruthless when it came to playing at cards. Any ambition he might have had in other fields had been diminished almost to nothing by the tribulations of his family. He would be a lord before long, but his family was so poor that he had been sent to sea when he was twelve, to avoid paying for his education.

The reason for his family's degradation, at least on his mother's side, was simple – the love of gambling – something Snowden had inherited. Since he was about five years old, he had devoted himself to it, not as a diversion, but with a single-minded determination to win. As a child he had watched people play in his parents' house and at the houses they visited in the neighbourhood. In his room, he had replayed those games, teaching himself to remember every card that he saw. He had studied players as they won and lost, and over time he had come to be able to read the small clues they gave away the cards they held, and learned to avoid giving away any clues about his own hand. He had learned to notice and to take advantage of every little thing, creases in the cards, stray reflections, and always to remain sober when those around were anything but. He found that he could recognise people who understood gaming, and he had learned to avoid playing with them, but to take advantage of those who had money but who were careless. He learned that to flaunt winnings or to boast of victory was to reduce the chances of more success, and even to court accusations of cheating.

In the last few years, aboard various men o' war in the long months of the blockade, he had practised endlessly by playing with his shipmates. He had been careful to play only for small stakes and not to win excessively, but nevertheless had honed his skills and tactics. He knew that it was true that luck in gambling could not be eliminated, and that sometimes he would lose, but he did his utmost to make luck as unimportant as possible.

And now was his opportunity to make good use of all the work he had put in, and it was going well. In Lymington and Weymouth his success was intentionally modest, but once they had got to France he had played for larger stakes. In St Malo the stakes were too large, he had overdone things, and there was a good deal of resentment. They had got out sharpish, and no harm was done. It had been a lesson in not pushing too hard, but he had got to Paris with gold coins in his pockets, riding his own horse, and found the city full of English society abroad for the first time in years, free from the inhibitions of life at home.

They found quite a reasonable house, with stables attached, and Snowden left Stone there and went to the British Embassy. *Nor now to prove our chance, longer will tarry.* He was in luck. As soon as he was admitted to the embassy and was in the process of being interviewed by a rather superior secretary by the name of Dennison, Lord Whitworth himself had come into the room, looked at Snowden and then at the secretary with his eyebrows raised quizzically. The secretary glanced at Snowden's calling card.

"The Hon Percy Snowden, my lord."

Whitworth, who was a handsome man, well dressed and with a commanding presence, asked, "Snowden, eh? Cornwall Snowdens by any chance?"

"Yes, my lord, my mother speaks highly of you."

"Does she? Bless her. Her situation not of the best, I suppose?"

The secretary handed Sausmarez's letter to Whitworth. "From Sausmarez in Guernsey, my lord."

Whitworth read the letter.

"He speaks highly of you, and especially this companion of yours, Stone. I've heard something of his exploits. We'd be in an even more tricky situation now if it wasn't for him. Well, look here, Snowden, I'll ask Dennison here to see if he can get you into something interesting one evening soon."

The secretary nodded, "Yes, my lord."

Whitworth hurried out and across the entrance hall, at the head of a small gaggle of clearly very important personages.

Dennison looked at Snowden, impressed no doubt with the preceding interview with his hierarch.

"I'm giving a little dinner tonight, at a room at the Palais Royale. You and Stone would be most welcome."

And that was how it had started, the most wonderful time of his life to date, which now seemed like a haze of happiness and pleasure.

The dinner with Dennison and his friends was pleasant, and had more or less seen Snowden and Stone accepted into the temporary society of English enjoying all that Paris had to offer. Most of the English visitors could hardly remember when travel to France had last been possible, and they knew that it couldn't last and were determined to make the best of whatever time they had.

They had spent many hours at the Palais Royale, a warren of shops, theatres, gambling houses and other less-reputable establishments, which was enjoying great temporary prosperity on account of the English presence. Snowden had played very little to start with, but soon was enjoying some success. He took care to vary the company he played with, and kept his winnings to a moderate level so that they were not remarked upon. There were, at the Palais Royale, men who made their living at the tables, and Snowden had soon learned to recognise their type and to avoid them.

Jack had accompanied him on most of his outings, and was rapidly becoming quite assured. Jack was popular on account of his exploits, which he was endlessly asked to relate, and, Snowden thought, also because of his frank and unreserved manner. His dress had improved after several visits to fashionable tailors and bootmakers.

About a week after their arrival, Stone and Snowden had been invited through Dennison to an evening gathering at a very elegant house with an even more elegant hostess, "owned", Snowden was told, by some high-up Frenchman. The room was a sea of colour, the women in extremely becoming muslin dresses. Snowden was talking to Stone when he noticed a group of distinguished-looking men moving to the side of the room and sitting down at a table to play cards.

"Excuse me, Jack, I think duty calls," Snowden said, and moved off to follow them.

Snowden had stood by the table, rather hesitant, wondering how best to get into the game, when one of the men looked up at him and said in excellent English, "Lieutenant Snowden, I believe. Would you like to join us?"

To say that Snowden was astonished that the man knew his name was to understate the case considerably, but Snowden recovered quickly.

"Snowden, yes, but only Midshipman, not Lieutenant. You have promoted me …."

"I think you will find that I have not. You are presumably not yet acquainted with the latest *Gazette*. I offer my congratulations."

He stood up and offered Snowden his hand, which he took.

"Charles Maurice de Talleyrand, at your service, and this is …." He went round the table, introducing the other players, who stood and offered Snowden their congratulations, but Snowden had been so shocked by this that he had taken no notice of their names. Here he was with the famous Talleyrand, minister of France, ally of Napoléon, and Talleyrand had just told Snowden that he had been promoted.

"You are very well informed, sir," Snowden stammered.

"It is essential that I am. You are from Cornwall, I understand."

"Yes, sir."

"As I thought. I believe I have had the pleasure of meeting your parents, in Falmouth. I spent some time in England during the revolution, but I was forced to leave by your government, and took ship to America. The ship was driven into Falmouth by the weather, and I took dinner with them at an inn. They had been in the town transacting some business I believe. We were joined by General Arnold – you have heard the name, no doubt. He and I were not particularly good company, I fear, he wishing to return to America and I desiring to avoid it at all costs, but it was a pleasant enough evening. … And now, to business."

They commenced to play. After his encounter with Talleyrand, Snowden had been in an extremely nervous condition, and drank a couple of glasses to steady his nerves. Talleyrand was a mesmerising conversationalist, extremely knowledgeable about the Royal Navy, and before long he had prompted Snowden to tell the story of his part in foiling the attempt to kidnap the King at Weymouth. Snowden got so taken up in the story that he hardly noticed that he had started to lose. He found out afterwards that Talleyrand had made a considerable fortune from gambling.

Probably it was the wine emboldening him, but he let slip to Talleyrand that the person mostly responsible for preventing the kidnap, Jack Stone, was in the room.

"Is that so?" said Talleyrand, though in hindsight Snowden was pretty sure he was aware of it already.

"Do you know whose house you are in, and whose wine you are drinking?"

"No, sir. I have some family connection to the ambassador, and we were invited as a result of that."

Talleyrand laughed. "You are in the house of Monsieur Morlaix, the commander of the raid."

Snowden thought that this was more than he could cope with in a single evening. He felt as though he had been kicked by a horse.

Talleyrand inclined his head, and Snowden looked in the direction he indicated.

"And furthermore, your companion, Stone, is in conversation with the daughter of Morlaix."

Indeed, Jack seemed to be getting on famously with a strikingly beautiful girl wearing a tricolour sash. Snowden was not sure that this was a relationship that should be allowed to flower.

"If you will excuse me, sir, I will go and speak with him."

"I think that would be a very good idea."

He started to rise, but Talleyrand held his sleeve and leaned towards him, speaking softly.

"I tell you this because I met your parents, and also because you are innocents, and Stone in particular is to be admired. Do not look now, young man, but in the corner of the room is one Fouché, our former chief of police. He is truly a man to be feared. He had a hand in planning the Weymouth raid, and I know that he did not take kindly to its failure."

He leaned closer. "I think that you are safe enough, but Fouché knows that Stone had no commission when he carried out his actions against France. I think you know the story of your Sidney Smith. There is peace now, but Fouché burns with resentment, and I advise you and Stone in all seriousness to leave France as soon as you can, before Fouché has Stone in the Temple, or worse."

Snowden stood up, suddenly sober.

"Thank you, sir, for your kind advice."

"My regards to your parents."

Snowden walked over to Jack, but could not resist glancing at Fouché, who happened to look up and hold his gaze. Snowden shivered.

Jack, who was engrossed in conversation with Mme Morlaix, was clearly very annoyed when Snowden drew him aside.

"We must leave, Jack."

And leave they did, at first light the following day, and two days later were at Harvre, taking ship for England.

Chapter 11 – Dominique

Dominique Morlaix thought that her parents were a strange pair, but nevertheless they were happy together. Her father could sometimes seem like a rough and ready Breton seaman, with an accent to match, and although this was indeed part of his personality, there was more to him than that. Practical ability, rather than the political kind, had made him useful to those in power, and kept him alive and even prospering during the long turbulent years.

In contrast, her mother was devoted to politics, and a consummate practitioner of its arts, using them ruthlessly to advance her husband's career. She was a true believer, from a political family. She had been at the storming of the Bastille, and had marched on Versailles, helping to drag a looted cannon. Dominique had been only a small child at the time, but she could still remember the shouting in the streets outside as her aunt, in whose care her mother had placed her, held her tightly, both of them trembling.

Her father had been away for long periods in her childhood. He was often at sea, or engaged in some service about which he did not talk much when he came home. During his absences, her mother had campaigned tirelessly on his behalf.

Dominique knew that her father had doubts about what he had done, and even about the First Consul. In contrast, her mother had no doubts about the Revolution, Republican France or Bonaparte. She was convinced that he was the man to protect what had been won.

Her mother was from the south, from free and easy Agen, and had not enjoyed living in Brittany. She disliked the Bretons' Royalist and Catholic sympathies, and hated the Chouans when the rebellion broke out. Her father was not like that, and had been horrified with the way that the uprising had been dealt with. Although he served the First Consul, it was with an air more of duty than anything approaching enthusiasm, and he was entirely too friendly with Talleyrand (the turncoat) for her mother's liking.

Dominique had no doubt that it was her duty to go to Brittany with her father. He had been in such danger leading the attempt to capture the English King. He had nearly succeeded, and it would have changed everything if he had. She hadn't been able to support him in that operation, but perhaps she could in Brittany. If the First Consul thought that there was important work for him to do there, she would go with him, and her mother could stay in Paris to attend to the politics.

It was not that Dominique was not enjoying life in Paris. She was, greatly. There was an exciting round of social occasions, she was a sought-after guest, and it was even more interesting now that there was peace and the English were here. That night, she had met a rather special Englishman, Jack. He was full of contradictions, and in some ways reminded her of her father. His command of French was rather hesitating, and he had an amusing accent, with almost peasant-like manners. His clothes were in good taste, though, and clearly expensive, and she saw a certain assurance, almost a swagger, behind his outward diffidence.

They had been getting along so well, and then his companion had spoken to him and they had almost fled from the house. She had seen the horrible Fouché look at Jack thoughtfully, and had wondered why he should take notice of a young Englishman.

In the morning her father called her into his room, and everything fell into place.

"The young Englishman you were speaking to last night."

"Jack. Father, what about him?"

"Yes, his name is Jack Stone. What I have to tell you is almost incredible, but seems to be true.   Dominique cast her eyes down. "He almost ran away last night. Fouché looked at him, and I knew something was not right."

"I told you of the attempt we made to take the English King."

"Indeed you did, father, and I am very proud of you, striking such a blow for the Republic."

"Rather aiming a blow, and missing."

"And now we have peace. Perhaps you taught the English a lesson."

"I have undoubtedly taught them much, and the problem is that they are quick to learn."

"Perhaps you will soon be teaching them something else."

"Perhaps so, but I am tired of fighting, and very glad that you will accompany me to Brittany, Chouans, Catholics and Royalists notwithstanding. Anyway, the boy, Jack." He looked closely at his daughter. "Did you know he was a naval man?"

"Of course I knew. You are my father, and I can recognise a seaman when I see one."

"You were right that Fouché was interested in him, and the reason for his interest is that Jack Stone was the chief reason that my raid on Weymouth failed. He is a remarkable young man, and that he has turned up in our house is more remarkable still, an astonishing coincidence, but turn up he did. Fouché was involved in planning the Weymouth raid, and had a great interest in it. I confess that my own feelings towards Jack Stone are not overly friendly, but Fouché bears him great animosity. You have some idea of what that means, especially as Stone was a civilian when he did the things he did. He does not have the protection in law that a regular sailor would have, though I am not sure that even that would be complete protection from Fouché."

Dominique shuddered, and her father, recognising her distress, spoke as comfortingly as he could.

"Ah, you see the problem. Don't worry too much. Talleyrand warned his companion, and if they have any sense they will have made themselves scarce."

BOOK 2 – WAR AGAIN
Chapter 1 – Blockade

Waterwitch was under short sail in the westerly gale, slowly forereaching away from the land in the huge waves, and everything aboard was damp. The galley fires had been extinguished by a particularly unpleasant breaker, and there was no hot food, leading to a certain feeling of resentment permeating the ship. Snowden stood on the poop deck in the rain, or rather clung to its windward rail, wondering if the scrap of sail the ship carried was too much for her. Losing a mast here could turn into a disaster, with the hellish Portsall rocks under her lee.

From time to time, through the rain to windward, he could just make out the bulk of Ushant and the seething breakers off the Brittany coast astern, and he had no doubt that they in turn were watched from the shore. A long way away, he watched a *chasse marée* emerge from the Trade, the channel inside Ushant, and rapidly run to the east, keeping close to the shore, almost amongst the Portsal rocks, knowing full well that the frigate was unable to intercept her.

Wilkinson, *Waterwitch*'s captain, emerged from the companionway and made his way towards Snowden across the slanting deck. Snowden nodded towards the French ship, far inshore, and Wilkinson nodded in return and attempted to focus his glass on it with one hand, the other being employed in clinging onto the taffrail.

"Good afternoon, Snowden. She'll be off to Rosco or Maloes no doubt, but we can't get anywhere near her in this."

"Sadly not, sir. Fast sailer it seems." Snowden remembered his trip with Stone from Dielette to St Malo in the *Rozzen*. Now *there* was a fast sailer. "I'm going back below. Call me if it gets any worse. Keep her heading north – I'd like a bit of sea room when the wind goes round to north-west, and that lot becomes a lee shore. Gives me nightmares." He indicated the maelstrom of white water south of the ship, around the rock they called the Four.

It did get worse, and Snowden did call the captain. Though the ship gained a bit more sea room, the night was one of intense struggle, and not one that Snowden thought he would forget readily. As the dawn light intensified, it revealed a dispiriting sight, though the weather had moderated, with the wind from the north-west and the sky clear. The jib boom was gone, trailing alongside, and the fore topmast was broken, hanging down in a tangle of rigging and sails. The ship was leaking as well, badly, and despite frantic searching in the night they had not been able to find the source, and the clanging of the pumps made a dismal sound.

As the ship rose on one of the immense swells, Snowden could see the white breakers around the rocks to leeward, perhaps two leagues distant.

Wilkinson looked at him with red-rimmed eyes. "Damned lucky not to have lost anyone."

"Smart work with those spars," reiterated Snowden.

"Thank you, sir. … Dennison," this to a seaman standing at a respectful distance, "Go below to the cabin and fetch up my spyglass."

"Aye aye, sir." Dennison disappeared, returning moments later with the captain's glass, handing it over gingerly.

"Thank you, Dennison," said Wilkinson to the seaman, who retreated to a respectful distance, close enough to respond quickly to any requests, but far enough away that he could not hear normal conversation. That was the idea, anyway.

The carpenter appeared. "Six feet in the well, sir, and I think the pumps are gaining on it slowly."

"Very well, Wills. What about the spars?"

"We'll get the jib boom back aboard directly, sir, but he's broken about halfway along. Reckon I can get him scarfed and run out again. We're trying to get the rigging and sails off the fore topmast and lower it down. Broken about halfway up it is, so I'll trim it shorter when it's on deck, and then we can run it back up and get the rigging set and that."

He gestured towards men working in the waist of the ship, and aloft on the foremast, surrounded by tangles of rigging and sails. Despite the huge swell left over from the gale, the jib boom was secured and about to be lifted back aboard.

"Tell the men we'll splice the mainbrace when that fore topmast is cleared away."

"Aye aye, sir." Wills went off to give the news to the men struggling with the spars.

At that moment there was a shout from the maintop: "On deck there. Three sail on the port quarter. Marys I reckon. Could be the ones we saw anchored yesterday."

'Marys' were what the sailors called any small French craft, a corruption of *chasse marée* or tide chaser. Yesterday they'd seen some ketches anchored close inshore at Camaret, and Snowden thought that Wilkinson had considered taking the boats in to them.

Wilkinson handed Snowden the glass. "Get up the mizzen shrouds and have a look round. I don't like the sound of that."

It was difficult to aim the glass with the rolling of the ship. Snowden leaned back against the ratlines, hooked one arm through a shroud and managed to adjust the telescope. The coast of Brittany swam into view, a seething mass of white in the foreground. He identified the Portsall rocks, and the black shape of the Four, and then, with a start, saw the sails of the three small ships the lookout had reported, leaving the Trade. They were not heading along the coast, as they usually did, but were close hauled under a press of sail, heading directly towards the frigate, occasionally obscured by rain showers.

"On deck there," shouted Snowden, above the roar of the wind. The captain looked up. "Heading towards us."

Seconds later, Wilkinson joined Snowden in the rigging, almost snatching the glass from him in his haste, and training it in the direction of Snowden's pointing arm.

"The ones we saw yesterday in Camaret. Bastards, they've seen we're dismasted and decided to take their chance. Keep an eye on them, Snowden."

He slid down the rigging with a grace belying his age and bulk.

The crew redoubled their efforts after a generous tot of rum, followed by breakfast, and the tempo of the pumps quickened.

Once the jib boom was back aboard, they set more sail on the main and mizzen masts, but the lack of jib boom and fore topmast meant that we could set no sails forward. The huge volume of water rushing around in the bilges made the ship roll awkwardly, but she began to make progress, desperately slowly, on the best course she could manage, parallel to the horrible lee shore of the Four and the Portsal rocks. The lack of foresails made the ship unbalanced, and from time to time she rounded up into the wind, sails thundering aback, and then she had to be coaxed round, back on course, losing ground and precious sea room, allowing the pursuing ships to close with her.

The crew's struggle to restore her rig, desperate enough on the pitching deck, was interrupted every time the frigate rounded up into the wind, and they had to leave the repair effort and work *Waterwitch* until she was under way again.

After an hour or so of this intermittent progress, the French pursuers were close enough for Snowden to make out every detail of them. They were small, fore and aft rigged, but the decks were crowded with men, and there were guns poking through the windward gunports. Through the glass, Snowden could make out the features of individual seamen as they crouched behind the bulwarks, sheltering from the spray thrown up by their dash through the seas.

Wilkinson, his hands gripping the weather taffrail as though to crush it under his fingers, turned to Snowden. "It's no good, Snowden, we've got to get her under control and take our chances with the French."

"Aye, sir."

Ten minutes later, *Waterwitch* was jogging slowly along under the main course and topsail, just about managing to keep her distance from the rocks along the coast. The French ships began to overhaul rapidly.   Snowden and Wilkinson watched as a series of flags broke out on the largest of the pursuers.

"Signalling," muttered Wilkinson, and was about to continue when he was interrupted by a shout from a lookout aloft: "Two sail on the starboard quarter," followed by "Hull down," and then "Frigates I reckon."

Snowden needed no urging, and was soon in the maintop with his glass trained in the direction indicated by the lookout.

They were frigates, two of them, wearing a press of sail, leaving the Four channel. They had probably come from Brest, alerted to the British frigate's difficulties by watchers on the coast. Snowden could just make out signal flags flying from one of them. He slid down the rigging and reported to Wilkinson, who grunted, "Back up and keep a good eye on them."

The first lieutenant, Hyde, arrived on the quarterdeck, dishevelled, dirty and tired looking after supervising the work forward. He discussed the situation for several minutes with Wilkinson and then shouted "Quarters!"

Waterwitch's progress was desperately slow, and the ketches were overhauling rapidly, two on her starboard side and one to port. After a while, the captain beckoned Snowden down and said, "Go and see how Hyde's doing. Chain shot, soon as he's ready."

Snowden went down to the gun deck and spoke to the first lieutenant. The men were at their guns, scarves around their heads to muffle the noise. Each gun captain had a long smoking match to hand.

"Captain's compliments, sir. When you're ready, chain shot."

Hyde, a taciturn Scot, nodded. "Aye, Percy, chain it is." He turned to the master gunner by his side. "Ye hear that?"

"Aye aye."

Snowden went with them as they walked together to the side of the ship, and peered out of a gunport, first on the larboard side and then crossing over and inspecting the two enemies rapidly becoming visible to starboard.

"As you bear, Guns, make 'em count."

The elderly master gunner crouched behind the aft gun on the starboard side, sighting along it and making small adjustments with wedges and handspike. He looked up at the gun captain, a young but very capable-looking man. "Wait, sonny, I'll give you the nod. She's got a bit of a roll on, so as she comes up." The frigate was indeed rolling, slowly, under the influence of the huge Atlantic swell last night's gale had generated, but with an odd, irregular rhythm caused by the water sloshing round in the bilge.

Apart from the noise of the wind in the rigging, and the sound of the frigate moving through the sea, the gun deck was hushed, with an almost unbearable air of tension. The men knew as well as Snowden that with *Waterwitch*'s damaged rigging and the water in the hold, any small damage that the ketches could inflict would reduce their chances of being able to clear the rocks to leeward, and increase the possibility that the pursuing enemy frigates could catch them before they were spotted by a blockading British ship. As a gambling man, Snowden didn't really like the odds. The enemy ketches were small, lightly armed, and completely outgunned by the frigate, but their aims were limited to one imperative – delay.

At that time, the Royal Navy had not quite achieved the complete assumption of victory against almost any odds that came after Trafalgar, but it was nevertheless spirited and confident. *Waterwitch* had had a successful cruise, with a steady succession of success and the capture of several lucrative prizes which had been sent back to England. She was well worked up, the crew highly trained and well led. "Just as well," Snowden thought to himself.

The frigate rolled slowly to starboard, held back by the weight of water in her bilges. Spray came in through the gunports. The gunner, still sighting along the gun's barrel, nodded and moved deftly aside as the gun captain touched the match to the hole in the breech and the gun fired with a deafening roar, flinging itself back on its ropes and filling the deck with smoke. The gun's crew threw themselves into action, sponging out and reloading with practiced speed.

Guns and the first lieutenant looked through the gunport at the French ketch, and then at each other, with a mutual slight shake of their heads. They moved to the next gun on the starboard side, and the procedure was repeated. After the third gun was fired, Snowden watched the French ketches start to bear away. The first lieutenant had noticed as well.

"Close!" he shouted to the guns. "Rattled, quick now."

"Starboard battery, as you bear, lads," shouted the gunner, and one by one the sixteen thirty-two-pounders fired, their noise, concussion and smoke overwhelming in the low-beamed space of the gun deck.

On the way up the companionway out of the gun deck, Snowden heard a cheer, and when he reached the quarterdeck he could see that the mainmast of one of the ketches on the starboard side had gone by the board and she was stopped in the water, men on her deck starting to cut at the wreckage with axes.

The other ketch was moving rapidly out of range, a broadside from *Waterwitch*'s starboard battery chasing her along, shot splashing all about her. Wilkinson and Snowden turned to look at the solitary French ketch on the port side, but while they were distracted, she had turned to starboard and was making apparently straight towards them, a dramatic sight, with a great white bow wave, leaning to her huge sails. Snowden's first thought was that she was going to the aid of her stricken companion, but he quickly realised she was going to try to sail close to the *Waterwitch*, under her stern, with the hope of a lucky shot taking down some rigging.

The port battery fired, a ragged broadside indicating that the guns were being individually sighted, but they could hardly bear and had no success. The ketch sailed on.

"Get the gunner up here," Wilkinson shouted to Snowden. "Smashers!"

The "smashers" were the carrons or carronades (short, stubby guns with a limited range, but which fired a devastating weight of metal) that Wilkinson, who had had considerable say in how the ship was armed during her commissioning in Portsmouth, had had installed, two on the quarterdeck and two on the foredeck.

"You men," he shouted directly to the crew of the quarterdeck. "Carrons."

"Canister."

The gunner arrived, smoke-blackened and out of breath.

"Shooting, Guns. Smashers now, cannister," cried Wilkinson.

The gunner nodded, "Bastards'll run right into them," and moved to the port carron and started adjusting its slide.

The French ketch was desperately close now, and began to fire, surprisingly accurately, with shot singing above the heads of the men on the quarterdeck. Holes appeared in the frigate's sails. All it would take for the ship to lose a mast was one lucky shot, and the odds would shorten.

The French captain was brave and determined, but the best Frenchmen have considerable, and sensible, respect for the carronade, and when he was perhaps fifty yards away he seemed to sense their presence and put his helm up, bearing away from the wind and the frigate.

Just too late. Snowden saw the men aboard her flatten themselves behind bulwarks, deckhouses and anything else that offered shelter, and with the ketch in irons, pointing into the wind with the sails flogging, the smasher fired.

The hundreds of balls swept across her deck, ploughing into the woodwork and cutting down men who had not managed to find shelter in time. Snowden heard screams and shouts, as the cutter fell back on its original course, stopped with the sails flogging, the helmsman probably dead or injured.

"Give her the other one," yelled Wilkinson, and the gunner moved to the starboard carron sighting along the barrel.

"Wooding," he shouted, meaning that part of the *Waterwitch* that was in the way of the shot.

"Fire, damn you," retorted Wilkinson, almost screaming.

The gun fired, and a good length of our own quarterdeck taffrail exploded as the balls tore through it, the remainder finding their way to the French ketch, whose mainsail came crashing down, the halyards shot through.

"I think that bastard'll leave us alone now," shouted Wilkinson in triumph to the gunner.

"I think he will, sir. Plucky Froggie though," replied the gunner.

Waterwitch ploughed on, desperately slowly, the Portsal rocks so close that the men on the *Waterwitch*'s deck almost seemed to look down on them as the ship rose on the swells.

"Snowden, come forward with me and we'll see how the work's going. We need those foremast staysails," said Wilkinson.

Snowden understood what he meant. The ship was sailing so slowly that not only were the French frigates overhauling them rapidly, but also *Waterwitch* was so hard to manoeuvre that she would be at a distinct disadvantage if it came to action.

The foredeck was a hive of activity when they got there.

The captain spoke to the first lieutenant. "My compliments, Mr Hyde, you seem to be making good progress."

"Thank you, sir. Desperate work, but Mr Wills has risen to the occasion."

Supervised by Wills the carpenter, the jib boom was being repaired, with men sawing, working with adzes, and the smith hammering at a forge which had been set up in the lee of some canvas sheets.

Wills turned to the captain. "Nearly there now, sir. Smith's going to put that last hoop just under the join, and that'll be the best we can do."

As they watched, the smith carried a cherry-red hot hoop of iron in a pair of pincers to the base of the jib boom and slid it up near the joint. As soon as it was in place an assistant poured a bucket of water over the hoop, which hissed and steamed.

"I think she'll hold, but try to treat her kindly, sir," said Wills, as the men started to carefully gather up the tools, and the smith threw water into the glowing coals of the forge and began to dismantle it.

Wilkinson looked at the join, which involved large screws, splints and turns of cord. "Looks effective to me, Wills. Perhaps not your most elegant work, but I suppose circumstances preclude that. Well done to you and your men. You seem to have worked a miracle."

"Thank you, sir. I'm off for a bathe now."

"Bathe, Wills?"

"Aye, in the bilges, looking for that leak. I reckon we've got a sprung strake somewhere near the waterline. Pumps'll uncover it soon perhaps if it isn't too deep."

He walked away, swaying slightly with fatigue, accompanied by the pumps' depressing sound.

Wilkinson beckoned the officers to him, and gestured astern, where they could see the remaining undamaged ketch shadowing the frigate, hanging well back, a huge tricolour snapping from her mainmast truck, and surprisingly, horribly close, setting all the canvas they could, the two chasing French frigates.

"They'll be up with us soon, but we're not finished yet, and I have a scheme to give them an unpleasant surprise."

As the French frigates relentlessly overhauled *Waterwitch*, her crew worked steadily to ready the jib boom, but kept the sails out of sight below. The forge was reinstated behind its canvas screen, and the smith worked noisily on some iron he brought up from below. Snowden hoped that from the pursing frigates, the repairs would look less advanced than they really were. The jib boom was rigged with a halyard on the end to lift it up, restraining shrouds, and a jackstay slack beneath it. The capstan was set up on an outhaul to winch it out. The work was delicate, ably supervised by Jones, the Master.

"Chance it'll work," he said to Snowden, and then at the top of his voice to a man balancing on the rail, "Careful there, I reckon Froggie won't stop to pick you up."

Snowden looked round. He'd been so engrossed in the work that it was a shock to see the two French frigates, only a few cable lengths away, one on each quarter.

"Damn close," he said, and ran aft to report to Wilkinson, who nodded.

Snowden went forward, and collected his boarders, who he had endlessly exercised under Wilkinson's supervision since joining the ship. He instructed them to crouch out of sight behind the bulwarks with their pikes, cutlasses and pistols at the ready. Snowden joined Jones, just as one of *Waterwitch*'s stern chasers fired, and a hole appeared in the mainsail of the ship on the port quarter.

"Good shooting," said Jones, and they turned back to the work. The frigates were now slightly abaft *Waterwitch*'s beam at extreme cannon range, ports open with their guns run out. They backed their topsails, slowing to keep pace with the frigate, but gradually decreasing the gap, waiting to pounce, but wary of their prey's ability to strike back.

Waterwitch's larboard broadside fired slow and deliberate, followed by the starboard one. Splashes appeared around the French frigates, but they made no reply, still edging closer. A few minutes later, the Frenchmen let their sails draw, surging ahead, sailing much faster than the crippled *Waterwitch*, almost stationary in the water. Snowden realised that Wilkinson had been right – they were intending to overtake the British ship, then alter course to cross her bows, pouring the full weight of their broadsides into *Waterwitch* while she was powerless to manoeuvre quickly and bring her own main armament to bear.

As the French frigates altered course to pass close ahead, Snowden stifled the urge to tell Jones, who to his mind seemed to be fussing unnecessarily with ropes and giving excessively detailed instructions to the men.

Jones broke the tension. "Ready now," he said, adding conversationally, "It might work."

Snowden nodded and waved to Wilkinson on the poop, who shouted "Now!" Men threw themselves in an ordered frenzy on halyard and outhaul, jackstay and brace, and the capstan turned, the pawl clacking. The jib boom moved out along the bowsprit, and the foretopmast stump began to make its way aloft.

After what seemed like only a few minutes of frantic activity, the foretopmast staysails were hoisted and sheeted home with a bang. *Waterwitch* started to come alive, her head paying off to leeward, and then the foresail was on her, men tallying on the braces, and she really started to move. Snowden went back to his boarders, and watched the foretopsail yard being swayed rapidly up, and then the topmen clambering onto it like monkeys to release the sail, which cracked and flogged before it was sheeted home. He dared not look aloft for fear of seeing the foretopmast bending or loosening, but *Waterwitch* was moving fast now with the helm up, heading directly towards the French frigate on the starboard side.

With the wind now on the quarter, *Waterwitch* heeled, picked up her skirts and ran wildly towards the French, the wake hissing along her sides. Marines, muskets on their backs, ran up the rigging to take their places in the tops.

For what seemed like a long time, the French carried on as though nothing had happened, although the hunted had rapidly become the hunter and they were suddenly in danger.

The captain yelled, "Stand by to repel boarders," and Snowden saw his men's hands tighten on their weapons, peering over the hammocks rolled on top of the bulwarks, ready. He looked up and saw the French frigate, now seeming almost close enough to touch, suddenly realising her danger, starting too late, much too late, to bear away. He saw ports in her stern thrown open and the muzzles of their stern chasers appear. *Waterwitch* altered course slightly to starboard, aiming for the French frigate's stern. The ships were so close. Close? It seemed that they were going to collide.

Snowden saw the other Frenchman to windward begin to wear ship, a cautious man he thought, too cautious for this sort of work. The gambler in Snowden shortened the odds in *Waterwitch's* favour. Standing on the foredeck, he looked up at the French frigate's poop, where men stared over the side, seemingly transfixed, horrified at the site of their suddenly living enemy, laden with doom, surging towards them.

From the corner of his eye, Snowden saw one of his men raise his pistol. He grabbed the man's arm. "Not now," he said, and the sailor put the pistol back in his belt, his eyes wild.

The British marines in the tops fired their muskets, and the French faces disappeared. The first gun of the larboard battery fired, the ball smashing into the stern gallery of the French frigate. The ships collided and then bounced apart again, and the stern of *Waterwitch* swung round towards the French frigate, which Snowden saw was called *Demoiselle*. A second gun fired, and then a third, sending thirty-two-pound balls through their stern gallery, and along the length of their ship, at gundeck level, doing God knew what damage to ship and men.

As *Waterwitch* slid slowly past *Demoiselle*, slowed by the entangling of the ships' yards, a cannon firing into her every minute, Snowden moved his boarding party aft, keeping abreast of her stern gallery, smashed to fragments by the British cannon. At last, after what seemed an eternity, the two ships stopped, held by a tangle of cordage, grinding together with a terrible grating noise. Snowden could see directly into the smoking ruin of the interior of the French ship.

Afterwards, Snowden couldn't recall exactly how it happened, but he thought he had looked round at the quarterdeck and saw, or imagined that he saw, Wilkinson raise his sword and point with it to the enemy.

Snowden heard himself shout, almost scream "Come on lads, after me," and then he was over *Waterwitch*'s bulwark, climbing into the shattered cabin of *Demoiselle*, slashing with his cutlass at a face that appeared in front of him, and running, running with his men behind him through the choking smoke into the ship, passing smashed and bleeding bodies and groaning, wounded men, and up the companionway onto the quarterdeck, yelling, screaming, firing his pistols and swinging his cutlass, and then over to the mizzen mast, slashing at the halyards until the tricolour was at his feet.

Snowden saw a French officer, one arm hanging limply, move towards him, and he raised his cutlass to strike at him when he felt a strong grip about him, pinioning his arms roughly into his side, forcing him to drop his cutlass to the deck with a clang.

"She's struck, sir," said the man holding him, a large marine in a tattered red coat. "It's over. Go and take his sword." And indeed, Snowden noticed for the first time that the French officer was holding out his sword, his eyes defeated, ashamed.

Chapter 2 – In Command

Later that day Snowden was standing on the poop of *Demoiselle* as she headed slowly east-north-east, away from Brittany and towards Guernsey, in command, he thought, through the fortunes of war, which are as fickle as those of gambling, not of a ship's boat, sloop or ketch, but of a fine frigate, or what had been a fine frigate until *Waterwitch* had set about her, raking her from end to end with a devastating broadside at point-blank range.

Intensely aware that she was vulnerable to the remaining French frigate, now bearing down to aid her stricken comrade, *Waterwitch*'s crew had fought desperately to escape from entanglement with *Demoiselle*. As the ships had separated, Wilkinson had sent a party of men and marines onto *Demoiselle* over the widening gap, shouting instructions to Snowden through a speaking trumpet, but it had been impossible to hear what he was saying as the distance increased, the ship's sails thundered as she laid off on the port tack, and the port battery fired a ragged broadside at the second French frigate.

Snowden had been so intent on his own work, securing *Demoiselle*'s shocked crew before they could recover sufficiently to realise that they outnumbered the boarders, and getting the ship underway, that he did not notice the undamaged French frigate suddenly turn away from the engagement and run as fast as she could towards France, the reason being the appearance on the northern horizon of two men o' war, obviously British.

And now those two ships, a frigate and a sloop, were up with *Demoiselle*, and had worn onto a parallel course. Guernsey was in sight, and *Demoiselle* was in as good order as they could get her for the time being, the wounded attended to by the surgeon's mates, the dead sewed up ready for burial, and the decks swabbed and guns secured. The ship's swivels had been loaded with grape and turned round to cover the maindeck. The ship's officers were detained in what remained of the great cabin, with armed marines at the door.

Snowden had felt exultation in close-quarter fighting, hand to hand with the enemy. He knew that it was not a Christian feeling, but he could not help himself. In the action he had become, literally, beside himself, as though he was existing outside of his body. He felt apprehensive before the action, but once it had commenced he felt no fear whatsoever. It is almost as though he had taken some drug, and afterwards he could hardly remember what he had done. After the action, this exultation quickly disappeared, and he felt drained, exhausted and depressed in spirits, and on this occasion even the thrill of his first command could not completely revive him.

The burial ceremony was not calculated to cheer, but it had to be performed. They did it as best they could with such ceremony as they could muster. The French first lieutenant read the words from their service as the English seamen stood in the waist of the windy maindeck, clasping their hats to their chests, while a few Frenchmen who had been allowed up for the occasion lowered their dead comrades into the rushing sea. When the last one had gone in, the French officer folded up the tricolour and handed it to Snowden, tears in his eyes. Snowden turned away from the dismal scene and climbed back towards the poop.

They anchored at St Peter's, under the guns of Castle Cornet. Snowden was heartily relieved.

Wilkinson came aboard from *Waterwitch.* "Well done, Snowden, but what the deuce were you thinking?"

"I don't know, sir, it wasn't a carefully considered plan, more or less spur of the moment."

"Through the stern gallery, I'll be dammed. Well done to your boarders. Didn't lose a single man either."

"No, sir. Lucky."

"Luck be damned. Saw your chance and took it." He looked round the French frigate, assessing her. "Nearly new by the look of her – fine vessel, very fine. Worth a pretty penny, or I'm a Dutchman." He rubbed his hands, thinking of the prize money. "Fine end to a cruise."

Her father came in late, as he often did, looking tired and worried, his clothes splashed with mud. He threw himself into a chair and took a long draft of the glass of cider which she handed to him. Behind him the cook appeared in the doorway and looked at Dominique enquiringly. Dominique nodded and she went off to prepare to serve the dinner.

"Bordering on the impossible, Dominique," he said, rubbing his hand across his face. "Bisset's a fine engineer, but he rubs the workers the wrong way. Energetic I grant you, but perhaps he's too young for the job. It's his first major project, and his boss hides in Paris, well out of the way."

He held up his hands, knowing that Dominique was about to say something in Bisset's defence.

"This morning there was a problem with the gates at Lock 13. They'd just got them swinging – you know what, they're absolutely huge, bloody miracle really – and they wouldn't quite close."

Dominique could imagine it very well, everyone tense, knowing that time before Bonaparte's visit "to inspect the completed works" was very tight.

"Well, Bisset starts to lay into Fournier – you know, the head mason – making out that the walls are not vertical, so the gates don't swing true." He shook his head. "And of course, this is at the top of his voice and with all the men listening, and so Fournier in turn attacks the carpenters who he claims are strangers to rulers and tapes. It really descends into a general shouting match, and so I climb down a ladder and get into a boat and start prodding around with a boathook. I think the masons are about to walk off the job, when I feel something with the hook, and manage to get the end of a waterlogged branch, almost a tree, up to the surface. It had obviously got between the gates."

He put his head into his arm, but started to laugh as he continued, "'Excuse me', I shout, 'excuse me', and lift the end of the branch out of the water. They all look down, and I say 'You masons and carpenters are all very well, but for serious work you need a seaman. Pass me a rope if any of you are capable of tying a knot'. Crisis averted."

The cook came into the room, announcing "Dinner is ready, citizens," and they moved into the small dining room.

Over dinner, her father continued to relay his woes.

"And then, in the sheds, they seem to be incapable of reading the drawings. I went in there this afternoon, and there is almost no sheer on the barges they are building now. Every wave of any size will wash right over the bow. The foreman says to me: 'Why do we need such sheer? The barges I built for the Midi Canal are flat decked, the sheer makes everything much more difficult, and the schedule is so tight'."

"Well, he's right there, isn't he, father?"

Dominique's father smiled at his daughter. "Whose side are you on?"

"It's just that the poor man does not understand what we are doing, does he? He built barges for the Canal du Midi, undoubtedly what he built worked well there, and he thinks that he should do the same thing again. He doesn't really know about the hundred miles of sea they're going to have to cross."

"Poor! If I had a quarter of his money I'd think myself very lucky, and he knows very well what we're about, they all do. Still, I suppose it wouldn't do any harm to have a quiet word."

I returned to Portsmouth, and joined the schooner *Clementine*, or what would be the *Clementine* when she was finished. She stood on the stocks, with activity all around her, but her planking was not even finished, and she was a long way off completion. Lieutenant Scoresby, who was to be her commander, lived with his wife in the town, and put in only infrequent appearances to inspect progress.

For the first few days I hung around the ship, with nothing whatever to do. To amuse myself I was in the habit of taking long walks around the bustling dockyard, and it was on one of these walks, late in the evening, that I met Robert Fulton.

I looked over the wall of a small wet dock at a man struggling with a line running over the stern of a rowing boat, wondering what he was doing. He looked up and shouted, "Can you row, boy?" in a pleasant American accent.

"Yes, sir, I can. Are you in need of assistance?"

"Indeed I am. Men have all gone, and we have visitors tomorrow. I have to place this," he indicated a large barrel-shaped object in the water astern of the boat, "in the middle of the dock, and I can't row and handle the lines at the same time."

I climbed down into the boat.

He held out his hand, rather muddy, and grasped mine firmly: "Robert Fulton, pleased to meet you."

"Jack Stone, pleased to meet you as well, sir. What is it?" I asked, indicating the barrel in the water.

"Torpedo."

This was not enlightening, as I had never heard of a torpedo, but Fulton, who always worked in a fury of energy, did not enlighten me, rather directing me at the oars. I spent the evening assisting him, laying out lines and generally preparing for what I gathered were to be important visitors.

It was getting dark as we finished.

"Thank you, Jack, you saved my hide there. Now the dockyard's so damned busy I cannot get the men. Come and dine with me."

"Thank you, sir."

As we walked back to his house in Southsea, I asked him what he was doing in Portsmouth.

"First of all, please call me Bob. I've had enough of your damned English formality. I've got some ideas which I'm working on for your navy. I was in France, but I have to say I don't agree with that Bonaparte, and to cut a long story short your government invited me here."

"Torpedoes?"

By now we were at Fulton's house.

"Jack, we'll continue the conversation at dinner."

The house was well kept and prosperous, the dinner was good, and I listened as Fulton explained what he was doing.

"The idea I'm working on for your navy is a torpedo. The ones I'm working on now are pretty simple, but the devil is in the detail. You float a barrel and sink it under the enemy ship, set the fuse, clear out, and then bang!"

I nodded.

"Of course, they can just be floated in among the enemy's shipping in port. Set off by clockwork or even a flintlock." He leaned closer. "As you're a serving officer, and my work is anyway rather public, I'll tell you that we're going to try something against Boney's invasion fleet in Boulogne."

A horrible suspicion was starting to form in my mind.

"Did you ever work on your torpedoes with the French?"

"Why yes. I was mostly working on the submarine of course, but did dabble with the torpedoes. The submarine could set torpedoes. Fifty pounds of powder in a barrel against the bottom of any ship will sink her. Even a first rate."

Submarine? I let that pass, and thought about the frigate *Iroise*'s pursuit of *Cicely* in the Channel.

"I think I may have been on the receiving end of one of your torpedoes."

Fulton gulped down his drink.

"I didn't make any for them."

"Well, you may have heard of the French attempt to take the King at Weymouth."

"Of course."

"I was in the frigate pursuing the ship which had been my ship before she was captured. I was trying to get away from Weymouth, and we had a very nasty encounter with something like what you are describing."

"Jack Stone, now I realise who you are. You were the lad that warned the King – toast of the country for quite a while."

"Yes, the French were intending to use torpedoes in the attack on Weymouth, but in the end used them on us. We realised what was about to happen at the last moment, but it was unpleasant. The powder was in barrels in boats."

"I'll wager I know why that was. Morlaix, I've been told he was the leader of that raid."

Morlaix – there was that name again.

Fulton continued, "I met him at demonstrations of my submarine I gave at Le Havre and Brest for the minister of marine, and afterwards in Paris. He's Boney's right-hand man. He looked at the drawing of the torpedo I was going to use with the submarine, and I knew by the questions he asked that he understood it immediately. I expect he went off and made his own. Not difficult for a man like that to make something rough and ready. So, Jack, we have a mutual acquaintance."

"More than you know."

I explained how I had gone to Paris with Snowden, and had been invited to Morlaix's house, the vision of Dominique coming into my head unwittingly as I spoke.

"Your friend Snowden did the right thing there, Jack, getting you to clear out straightaway. That Fouché is a nasty piece of work. Very bad reputation."

I spent the rest of the evening with Fulton as he explained his ideas, which to me were intensely interesting. I had no idea that the things of which he spoke were possible. He had spent hours completely underwater in a submersible vessel, and was a great admirer of a man who I had never heard of, James Watt, who had developed a steam engine which Fulton had adapted to propel a boat. He was a great advocate of canals, and we discussed the canal I had seen being built in Brittany.

"Whenever there's a canal, the trade of the places it passes through increases. I know Bridgewater, and his canal has changed Manchester beyond recognition."

As I rose to leave, Fulton said, "Jack, you've been a great help to me tonight, and as your ship is not ready for you, what would you say if I had a word with the hierarchs and got you seconded to me until she's finished?"

Thus started my interest in science and engineering, an interest that has subsequently come to dominate my life.

The three months I spent with Fulton at Portsmouth were probably the most interesting time of my life. My life in the Navy, and even my time in France, could be related to things I had previously experienced, or had known of. Working with Fulton was entirely different. I was plunged into a world of which I had no knowledge whatsoever, and which I had not known had existed, or even could exist.

True, the navigation that I was beginning to learn was based on science, mathematics and astronomy, and the instruments we used were very finely made, but they just allowed me to do the things I did already, though with greater certainty and precision. In contrast, the ideas of Fulton – submarines and especially steam engines – were utterly unknown to me beforehand. I had had no idea whatsoever that an underwater vessel could exist, that water could be pumped from mines using the heat from coal, and far less that steam could be made to push ships along against the wind. But these things were possible and did exist, and in some parts of the country steam engines and wondrous machinery were already commonplace. I was working with a man, Fulton, who had actually built a steamboat and a submarine.

With the exception perhaps of Morlaix, who might have been his equal, Fulton was the most accomplished man I have ever met, and working with him was an astonishing experience. We worked all day, from early morning until late at night, sometimes in his office, drawing, sometimes in workshops, but most frequently outside in the yard, or afloat. It seemed he could do anything. He could make a drawing of a machine quickly, and so clearly that its purpose and design were immediately apparent; he could work with tools as well as his experienced craftsmen, and could handle boats and rigging with practiced ease.

From time to time I passed the schooner, and watched as her hull was finished. One day I noticed that she was no longer on the stocks, but had been launched and warped round to the mast pond, where sheerlegs were in action, stepping her masts. Before long, she was in the fitting-out basin, and it was obvious that my time with Fulton was coming to an end.

My time ended, appropriately enough, with a bang, a very impressive one. Before a large and important gathering of Navy men, we exploded a torpedo under the hull of a small ship anchored at Spithead, breaking her clean in half and causing her to sink rapidly. The Navy was planning to use Fulton's weapons – "infernal machines" he called them – against Bonaparte's invasion fleet in Boulogne, and there was considerable interest from people in high places about his progress.

On my way to join the schooner, by now fully crewed and almost ready for sea, I stopped off to say farewell to Fulton.

"Jack," he said, "I expect I'll be back in America before long, there's plenty of scope for my steamers on the rivers there. If you're ever in that part of the world, come and look me up. There'll always be a job for you if you've had enough of the Navy."

We shook hands, and I walked over to *Clementine* and stepped aboard.

I saw Sausmarez in the sternsheets of a rather ornate barge as it was rowed under the stern of *Clementine*, the schooner that I had joined as midshipman in Portsmouth a few months earlier, and which was now lying in the roadstead of St Peter's in Guernsey. As *Clementine* was attached to Sausmarez's Channel Islands squadron, I had come across him from time to time, but we had never spoken. This was hardly surprising, given the enormous disparity in our ranks. He looked up, saw me, nodded and touched his hat. I saluted in return and watched as the barge went alongside the Channel Islands' flagship, the frigate *Hera*, and Sausmarez climbed aboard, accompanied by a crescendo of whistles.

Lieutenant Scoresby, *Clementine*'s commander, was already aboard *Hera*. The packet boat, which had just arrived from England, lay alongside the quay.

George Roberts, *Clementine*'s other midshipman, looked at the scene on the flagship and then at me. "Action now, Jack?"

"I wouldn't be surprised, George. Must have been something in the despatches, and now there's a conference going on." I looked up at the sky. "Dirty weather about as well."

About an hour later we heard a gun fired on the frigate, and watched as her foretopmast staysail was loosed and allowed to flap slowly in the breeze, a signal well known to all seamen.

"Prepare to sail," cried Roberts.

As he spoke, Baird, the first lieutenant, appeared on deck and looked towards the frigate as a hoist of signals appeared on her mizzen mast.

"That's 134, 'PREPARE FOR SAILING'," shouted Roberts.

"I'm only a yard from you, Roberts," retorted Baird. "No need to shout."

"Sorry, sir."

"Don't apologise, just acknowledge the signal."

"Yes, sir." Roberts ran off to the mast to hoist the acknowledgement.

By this time our schooner was a hive of activity, men appearing on deck from every hatchway and looking towards the flagship, where the smoke from the gun was clearing. They knew without being told what the gun and loose foretopmast staysail meant. There were hardly any orders given as the ship was made ready for sea, men tramping round the capstan, loosening sails, and securing the boats. There was a shout of "Boat approaching," and we saw *Clementine*'s launch coming towards us, the men bending to their oars with a will.

The master, Carré, came onto the poop deck. "Up and down, all ready," he said to the first lieutenant, meaning that the anchor cable was hauled in short and the ship was ready for sea.

With a start, I saw that Sausmarez was sitting beside our captain in the launch's sternsheets.

"Sir," I shouted to the first lieutenant, and pointed.

"Admiral's coming aboard."

The first lieutenant swore, the master swore, and then rushed down to the maindeck, pushing the men into some sort of order ready to greet the admiral.

An hour later we were at sea, heading south, and I was sitting with Roberts in the midshipmen's berth.

"Off to Maloes, apparently," he said. "Master told me we're just going to have a look round."

"Why?" I asked.

"Must have been a despatch from England. You know what they're like worrying about big bad Boney." In the Navy, the population of England was derided as being unduly worried about the French invading, though it was not perhaps such an idle fear as we made out. The Channel was big, and all Bonaparte needed was a moment of inattention from the British Navy. We all knew of the previous French attempts at invasion, and how close some of them had come to success.

Roberts continued, "I don't understand the presence of our esteemed admiral, though."

I thought I did. "The Old Man's pretty new to this station, and I think Sausmarez has come as pilot." Sausmarez's ability to find his way around the Channel Islands and the adjacent French coast was legendary in the Navy.

Clementine forged slowly through the pitch-black night, her foresails aback and just visible as shadows against the starry sky. I was in the chains, with Carré the master, Sausmarez, and Jean Breton his coxswain, all Guernseymen. A master's mate hanging over the side cast the lead into the sea, paying out its rope as it sank to the bottom.

"And a half, sixteen," he intoned, indicating that there were sixteen and a half fathoms of water.

The master's mate retrieved the lead and held it upside down in the light of a lantern held by a seaman. Its base, which had been coated in tallow, had collected a sample of the seabed, and the three Guernseymen gathered round, closely examining it and pinching bits of sand and shell between their fingers. They spoke in the strange mixture of what I knew to be Norman French and English, which I had heard before in Guernsey.

"You're right, your honour," said Breton.

"Just off Banchenou."

"What say you, Carré?" said Sausmarez to his coxswain.

Carré nodded. "I reckon. We'd see the light on Fréhel easy, if it was burning." This was a reference to what my *Petit Neptune* described as a "remarkable light-house", but which the French had extinguished on the outbreak of hostilities.

The conference was interrupted by a shout from the foretop lookout: "Breakers two points on the larboard bow."

"Up there and take a look, Mr Stone," said Sausmarez. "It should be an isolated rock."

I ran up the foremast rigging as the leadsman shouted out, "By the mark, fifteen."

I arrived at the foretop, and the lookout, a very young man no doubt chosen for the excellence of his vision, pointed towards where he had seen the breakers. I peered through the blackness, and after a few minutes saw the white flash of a breaking wave.

"Good work," I said to the lookout, and descended to find the Guernseymen again examining the lead.

"Looks like an isolated rock, sir," I said to Sausmarez.

Sausmarez shouted towards the poop, "We're just off Banchenou, Scoresby. As she goes now, and a sharp lookout, if you please. We'll let her run for ten minutes."

Sausmarez inverted a ten-minute glass and looked at it closely as the ship ran on, shouting to the poop when the glass ran out.

"Bring her to, Scoresby. We'll have another cast."

There was a scurrying of men, the ship slowed, the lead was cast again.

"By the deep, thirteen."

The conference around the base of the lead reconvened while the ship lay almost absolutely quiet, except for a low moan from the wind in the rigging and the occasional creak from the hull to break the silence. In the darkness astern, I heard the suck of surf on the rocks.

The conference came to a conclusion, and Sausmarez set off towards the stern of the ship, beckoning for me to follow. We joined Scoresby in the cabin and examined the chart.

Sausmarez indicated a place on the chart. "About here I think, Scoresby. Mark it, if you please, Stone. Set a bit to the west, but the reckoning's not bad," Sausmarez added, indicating a line on the chart, which recorded our estimated position, based on the record of estimates of speed and course.

"Thank you, sir," said Scoresby.

"Wants about an hour of high water?"

"Yes, sir, that's about right."

"I want to be here," Sausmarez indicated a position on the chart, a couple of miles off the French coast, a coast seemingly made impenetrable by innumerable rocks, "At dawn. The Passage des Decollees will give no trouble around high water. Alter to east-south-east, if you please, Scoresby, and a sharp lookout."

I knew from my reading of the *Petit Neptune* that a ship following the Passage des Decollees, which Sausmarez was proposing to take, would follow the French coast closely for a couple of miles, before entering the Rance estuary, just opposite the town of St Malo. I also knew that the *Neptune* described the passage as "*very difficult, and frequented by none but small vessels*".

The ship ran on slowly through the night, with the leadsman shouting out the soundings, and the seabed committee examining the samples which it brought up. With the dawn, the ship's company went to quarters, quietly, with what orders were necessary given in whispers, and *Clementine*'s somewhat unimpressive weaponry was readied, but not run out.

We slowly became aware of the stars dimming, and shortly there was a cry from the masthead, "Land on the starboard bow."

Sausmarez walked briskly to the foremast, followed by Carré. Scoresby turned to me. "Into the cabin, Stone, pick up a slate and chalk, and up into the foretop. He'll want you to take notes, or even sketch."

When I joined Sausmarez at the masthead, I could see the town of St Malo ahead, and the rigging of ships in the harbour and roadstead, but Sausmarez and Carré were focused on the channel which the ship had to navigate, often conferring. Sinister-looking broken water was all around, and the ship was moving quickly with the tide. From time to time Sausmarez would shout an alteration of course to the poop deck, and Bouchard, who had taken the helm himself, would give the ship a spoke or two of wheel. Men trimmed the sails as the ship swung, almost without orders.

The ship sped along, and was just passing the last line of broken water, almost in the clear, when she bumped hard on a rock, sending tremors through the rigging. We hung closely to the ropes as the ship started to slew broadside to the tide and to heel violently. I felt the shocks as the ship dragged her keel over the rocky seabed below, and I could hear Sausmarez softly alternately cursing and encouraging the ship. I was mentally preparing myself for the worst, for the ship to come to a standstill, a few yards from the French shore, but to my immense relief the bumping stopped, and she righted herself and was swept into the roadstead of St Malo, the town and harbour open just ahead.

Sausmarez passed his hand over his brow. "That was unpleasant. Damned close-run thing."

"Yes, sir," I answered.

"Let's have a look at the place, and get out."

His focus shifted from conning the ship to the view ahead. "A lot of ships in there, Stone," he said, peering through his glass.

"Yes, sir."

A seaman ran rapidly up the rigging and addressed Sausmarez. "Captain's compliments, your honour. He says to tell you the ship seems to be tight, and answering normally."

"Thank you. My compliments to the Captain also. Ask him to shorten sail and take us close to the harbour."

"Thank God for that," he added, as he trained his glass on the town.   "Carré, go down and point out the Rance Stone beacon to the commander."

"Aye, sir," and Carré descended.

By now we were only a cable's length from the town. I could clearly see the hotel where Snowden had had such success at the tables, and even the steps where we had taken the boat for our passage to Dinan. It looked so peaceful that I could hardly believe that it was the town of our enemy.

"Count the ships, Stone."

I did as I was told, and made notes of their number and type.

"I can see no barges, Stone."

"No, sir."

"Do you see any barges, lookout?"

"No, your honour."

And indeed, I could see none of the flat-bottom barges of the type the French had built at Boulogne recently with the intention of carrying their army to England.

"Several frigates, though."

"Yes, sir."

"No sign of any boatbuilding as far as I can see. Tides on the stand," meaning that the tide was high and would shortly be flowing out of the estuary.

"Boat approaching, sir," cried the lookout, pointing to a boat being energetically rowed towards us.

There was an indecipherable hail from the approaching boat, answered by a reply in rapid French from Bouchard at the wheel. The boat was rowed away as energetically as it had approached, and a man stood up in her, shouting to people ashore.

"That's it then," said Sausmarez. "Guernsey accent gave it away. Best get going before Frog gathers his wits."

It looked to me as though Frog was already starting to gather his wits, impressively quickly. Men were running, and I could hear orders being shouted. Flags broke out above the fort. Men, soldiers, some of them wearing tall shakoes, some hatless, and some half-dressed, ran to the quayside, knelt and primed their muskets.

Sausmarez hailed the quarterdeck. "Gybe her round, Scoresby, quick as you like. Let's get out."

The men ashore began to fire. The range was extreme, perhaps a cable's length, but there were a lot of men, clearly soldiers, and balls started to whizz around the ship, some of them striking the timber with a thud. *Clementine* gybed, the great booms sweeping above the deck as she came round and stood out to sea. The men cheered, and I looked up and saw that the colours had been hoisted. *Clementine* fired her rather puny broadside, and the men cheered again. I saw Sausmarez climbing down from the foretop, making his way to the poop.

Men climbed into the tops, releasing the topsails, while others on the deck braced them home. The ship responded, heeling, the town sliding quickly past. As the smoke of battle drifted across the land, I briefly glimpsed, in the gap between two buildings, a strange vessel moored in a small dock. I only saw her for a moment, wreathed in smoke, but she seemed to be about sixty feet long, with squared off ends and numerous oar holes in her sides. I noted her particulars down, just as the guns in the fort started to fire. The first shot sent a hissing swarm of grapeshot over the men on the poop, but the second and then the third fell short.

The men cheered as *Clementine*'s broadside crashed out again. There was a gust of wind, and the ship heeled violently, throwing up a great wake, and when I glanced back the town was behind us. I looked towards the open sea. On the starboard bow, at the end of the passage, I could see the heavily fortified islands guarding the main channel into the port, and at the end, Cézembre Island. The lookout and I simultaneously saw four galleys leave Cézembre's little harbour and make their way as quickly as they could be rowed to intercept us.

I hailed the quarterdeck. "Galleys leaving Cézembre, rowing quickly."

From my high vantage point, I could see soldiers moving rapidly around in the fort on the second island, Petit Bey. We swept past the fort, pretty close, and its guns fired. I heard the balls whistle overhead, and one struck the side of the ship. Good shooting, but then they had had plenty of time to practise for just this eventuality. Our puny broadside fired again in exchange, but the chances of it doing any serious damage against a stone fort were remote.

The galleys were slowing as they reached the middle of the main channel, waiting for us. I looked at them with concern – it was not likely that *Clementine* could prevail against four galleys, armed with heavy swivels in their bows and packed with boarders. I should not have worried, for *Clementine*'s helm was put down, and we slid close under Le Petit Bey fort, its guns still firing, and raced along the English Passage to the east with all sail set, at a much greater speed than the galleys could hope to achieve.

By dawn the next day we were anchored at St Peter's.

It had been a struggle, severe at times and taxing, but at last the canal was open, at least when the locks worked as they should. Morlaix felt elated, perhaps not quite so much as Bisset, the young engineer, but nevertheless very cheerful. This happiness was not because Morlaix knew that Bonaparte would praise him when he visited in a few days – he was inured to Bonaparte's praises – but because he felt a sense of achievement.

Perhaps Morlaix's intentions for the canal were warlike and impure, but Rennes was now connected to the sea. The canal would outlast the war, and Morlaix was sure that in years to come, when conflict was a distant memory, the waterway would be of great benefit to the prosperity of Brittany, so lamentably reduced after the years of turmoil and strife. Before long, the canal would stretch in the other direction, to Biscay, connecting the two seas.

Morlaix reflected that he had helped to do something that was worth doing. He had seen the benefits that the first canal, now called Le Midi, had done for the towns along its course, and even for the great city of Toulouse. Trade had increased, and agriculture and industries had prospered. It was said that the same was true of the town of Manchester in England.

On horseback, Morlaix had followed the barge loaded with soldiers as it made its way along the canal, and watched from a sloop on the Rance as it emerged from the last lock. Oars appeared at its side and a small sail was set. The sloop followed the barge as it was caught in the ebb tide, and before long the troops were disembarked at St Malo and made their way to their quarters in the fort.

Morlaix was the guest of the commandant of the fort, and at dinner the discussion turned to the arrangement for the trials. On the following day, the barge would be loaded with ballast to represent the weight of the men she was to carry, and she would be rowed and sailed into the open sea to assess her performance. After this, on the following days, troops would be embarked and the men made familiar with their duties aboard, and eventually there would be practice landings on the beaches of St Malo. Morlaix was sure that this was crucial to the success of the operation, and he was determined not to be rushed by Bonaparte.

After dinner, Morlaix walked along the ramparts of St Malo, looking out over La Manche, to the north, to England. He knew that the distance was much greater than that from Boulogne, but the English would not be expecting an approach from St Malo. The English blockaded Brest and Ushant, and the narrows around the Dover Strait, but their forces were weak in between, and that was something the French could exploit. Their Channel Islands' squadron was feeble, and Morlaix believed that there were sufficient French forces, if concentrated, to prevent its interference with the invasion fleet. The barges themselves would be secure from the English Navy, as they were not, as at Boulogne, right on the shore, but miles from the sea at Rennes. Could a more unlikely location for an invasion fleet against England be conceived than Rennes? The lake being created with dams would enable them to practise manoeuvring the barges, and landing from them, far from the attentions of the English. Perhaps, later in the programme, they could be taken in small batches for exercise at St Malo so that they could experience the way of the barges at sea.

Morlaix reviewed the outline of the plan in his head. During a spell of south-westerly weather, the troops would embark on the barges, take them down the canal to Dinan, and then strike out boldly for England, protected by the warships that would be assembled at St Malo. Some barges would divert to secure the Channel Islands, but most would land in England, at night, and establish a foothold on the enemy's territory. Morlaix was not entirely convinced that the foothold, once gained, would be easily held, as the English song had it:

They say they'll invade us, these terrible foes,
They frighten our women, our children, our beaus,
But if they in their flat-bottoms, in darkness set oar,
Still Britons they'll find to receive them on shore.

However, Bonaparte believed he could conquer England in this way, and Morlaix thought that an army could be landed there, given good weather and good luck. He was less sure that this would result in the conquest of England. He had seen what had happened in Egypt.

He walked around to where the barge lay, checked its moorings and spoke to the men guarding it, then went to bed, where he slept uneasily.

Morlaix was awakened in what seemed like no time at all by a great tumult of shouting. He ran out of his room and onto the ramparts, and asked a naval officer, who was staring into the roadstead, what was happening. The officer raised his arm and pointed.

"There, citizen, an English ship."

There she was, just off the town, a large armed schooner, unmistakably English, entering the Rance from the Passage des Decollees, narrow and rock strewn as it was. It was not something Morlaix would have liked to try, but the schooner had made it. There were men in her foretop looking down at the town, and men on the poop, training their spyglasses ashore. There was no doubt that the schooner's mission was one of reconnaissance, and from Morlaix's point of view she had picked a bad time to do it.

At that moment, the few guns in the fort which could be brought to bear fired, and Morlaix saw holes appear in the English ship's sails. Too high, but good shooting; he would congratulate the gunners later. A man climbed down from the foretop and ran to the poop. As soon as he got there the schooner gybed all standing. There was a cheer from the ship as a blue English ensign broke out at her main peak and a blue pennant on the foretop. The topsails were loosed, and she heeled as she stood out to sea.

Morlaix realised with a start what the blue pennant meant, that there was an Admiral aboard, and ran into the fort and up to the seaward battery. He grabbed the lieutenant of artillery standing by the guns.

"Grapeshot, quickly."

The lieutenant gave the orders, and his men rushed to respond, reloading their guns. Morlaix snatched his glass out of his hand, and at that moment the ship sailed past, close and fast, just under the guns. In a moment, she'd be gone. He saw the name on her stern, *Clementine*, and the blue flags.

He shouted to the lieutenant, "Sweep the poop deck, quick as you can." The ship was nearly past the fort.

A gun captain shouted that his cannon was ready, and the lieutenant ran over, sighted along the barrel and nodded. The gun fired, and through the glass Morlaix saw men on the ship's poop duck as the shot went over, splashes appearing in the sea as it fell just over her.

The next gun fired, and the next, but the shot fell short. The moment had passed. The ship clearly saw the galleys putting out from Sezembre, and turned violently to starboard, heading out along the apply named Passage des Anglais. Morlaix heard the Petit Bey guns firing, but he knew they would have to be very lucky to hit a ship sailing so fast. They were not lucky, and he watched as *Clementine* – "*HMS Clementine*", he thought – headed out to sea. He handed the lieutenant's glass back to him.

"Good shooting, lieutenant, I think you have just given their Admiral Sausmarez a scare."

"Admiral Sausmarez, sir?"

But Morlaix had turned and was walking away. Sausmarez. He had realised immediately he saw her that the schooner's intent had been reconnaissance, and clearly she was in the charge of an audacious seaman, one with local knowledge. Though the ship was small and insignificant, the blue pennant which broke out when she was discovered meant that she had an admiral of the blue aboard. Sausmarez, from Guernsey, and probably in charge of the squadron there, would know St Malo, and he had a reputation for daring. Indeed, Morlaix believed that he had narrowly avoided his ships when he had returned from Egypt with Napoléon.

What had the English seen? They had undoubtedly counted the ships in the harbour and in the Rance, and had noted the state of readiness of the garrison, but Morlaix thought it unlikely that in the crowd of vessels there, and in their sudden turn seawards, they would have noticed the barge, which was in any case partly concealed behind a bastion. He reasoned it away, but he was left with a nagging sense of unease.

It was a fine morning, the sun quickly burning off a low mist clinging to the sea's still surface, when Snowden stepped onto the quarterdeck of "his" ship, the French frigate *Demoiselle.* He was to be her commander until she was repaired sufficiently to allow her to sail to Portsmouth, where she would be assessed as a prize and repaired, but his proprietorial feelings ran deeper than his command of her. He felt as he did after he had won at cards. The French had had a strong hand and had played it badly. The English had been dealt a bad hand, but had played it boldly and skilfully. Snowden had played a decisive part in taking the frigate, and the prize was his.

He had a feeling of great satisfaction, and breathed deeply as he looked round the roadstead, the anchored ships mirrored in the calm sea. *Clementine* had returned from St Malo, apparently undamaged except for some ragged holes in the sails, which the crew were sending down for repair. Lucky – that was what they said about Sausmarez. Perhaps he was, Snowden thought, but he was one who made his own luck.

As he watched the admiral's barge put out from the quay and ferry Sausmarez and his entourage ashore, he had an idea. Temporarily he was commander of a large man o' war, and he didn't see why he shouldn't take advantage of that brief eminence. He went down to the cabin, which still bore some of the scars from *Waterwitch*'s broadside, sat down at the desk, and wrote a note inviting Jack to dinner aboard *Demoiselle* that evening. For the sake of propriety, he addressed the note to Scoresby, *Clementine*'s commander, inviting him as well, adding as a postscript "you may be assured of some fine claret with your dinner, lately the property of officers of the French Marine".

Later that morning he received a reply, informing him that Scoresby regretted that he would be unable to attend as he was invited to the Admiral's house, but that Midshipman Stone would be delighted to accept. At other times, he might have felt a twinge of jealousy that Scoresby was dining with the Admiral, and moreover most likely with his daughters, but he felt that showing Stone the ship he had captured and brought to Guernsey would more than compensate.

At the appointed hour, he watched a small boat put off from *Clementine* with two people aboard, and before long Jack's head appeared at the top of *Demoiselle*'s accommodation ladder, accompanied by a young man who Jack introduced as George Roberts, *Clementine*'s other midshipman. As Snowden showed them round the ship, he joked that Jack always preferred to row himself. The ship was by now pretty well cleared up, though there was not much of a crew aboard. Jack and Roberts were suitably impressed, and Roberts urged Snowden to describe the capture of the ship. As Snowden related the devastation *Waterwitch*'s broadside had wrought when it had raked the *Demoiselle*, he realised that Jack's usual distaste at accounts of fighting had become more acute, and this was confirmed when he said, "A famous victory," and Snowden knew that he was quoting Southey's poem about the Battle of Blenheim.

The dinner in the great cabin was cheerful, with Roberts pressing Snowden on the value of the ship and the likely prize money.

Jack told them about *Clementine*'s visit to St Malo. "Sausmarez is really astonishing, the way he found his way into St Malo. Hit pretty hard on the rocks off Dinard, I mean less than a cable's length off Dinard, but we made it and were in the roadstead as it got light."

"What was it like – anything interesting?"

"Well, there were a lot more soldiers around than when we were there, and quite a few warships in the harbour. I was in the foretop, with Sausmarez, almost looking down into the town. Things got pretty busy and we left directly we were spotted, and the fort at the end of the town had a few shots at us."

"Why is Sausmarez so interested?"

"It's because he's worried about Froggie taking the Channel Islands and using them as a base against us."

As they sat at their wine after dinner in the cabin of Snowden's ship, he felt admiration for the fine taste of her former officers, who certainly knew how to pick a vintage. He thought it might even have been appreciated by Jack, who was really a terrible philistine.

Jack spoke of his time in Portsmouth with the American, Fulton, which had impressed him greatly, and talked of torpedoes. Roberts and Snowden were sceptical, but Jack would brook no opposition. He looked at Snowden. "You may scoff, but you've had direct experience of them, Perce. Remember when we were chasing Morlaix when he was in the *Cicely*?"

Snowden nodded, remembering only too well.

"In particular, do you remember the boat full of powder?"

"My ears still ring from it."

"That was one of Fulton's torpedoes. It was meant for the frigates in Weymouth Bay. They didn't get the opportunity to use it in Weymouth, but tried it against us."

"Nearly got us, as well."

"It did. But Fulton's got plans for torpedoes, bombs, which are anchored underwater and explode when a ship touches them, or they can be set off by a clockwork."

"I helped in one of his expositions, and we sank a brig at Spithead. Bang, it was gone, in pieces."

"There's a plan to use them against the French barges at Boulogne." Jack went on to explain how Fulton had built a submarine boat that could plunge underwater and stay submerged for several hours.

"He's got a way of propelling it underwater without oars. It can go as fast underwater as a boat can be rowed on the surface. He built one at Rouen and then a better one at Brest. Morlaix was at the exposition at Brest. Fulton had a falling out with Boney, and we recruited him to come here and work for us."

Jack really seemed to have come alive as he described Fulton's work. "The most impressive thing, though, is the steamboat"

Roberts looked confused, and Snowden didn't think that it was just the claret.

"Steamboat?"

Jack leaned forward. "Yes, that is what will change the world. Fulton built one at Paris, sixty feet long or so, and it went against the current on the Seine."

Snowden could see that Roberts was completely lost.

"If the French had taken him up on the idea, all they would have had to do was to wait for a calm day, when our ships couldn't move, and use steamboats to tow the barges to England. And now, he's friendly with James Watt."

Snowden had never heard of Watt, but listened as Jack explained how Watt had made a much improved steam engine, and was making a great business of these engines with a man called Boulton.

"And canals as well. Fulton's a great exponent of canals. I've seen drawings he's made of his ideas for them, with the barges pulled by steamboats, and the barges made so they fit exactly into the locks."

Snowden said, partly to get Stone away from the subject of Fulton, about which he thought he was becoming rather obsessed, "Do you remember the canal we saw that Froggie was building near Rennes? All those buildings. They must be turning out a rare number of barges by now."

The talk drifted off into reminiscence of their time in France, with Roberts' eyes almost popping at their description of the Palais Royal, but Snowden could see that Jack was thinking deeply about something.

"What is it Jack?"

"It's something you said just now, about the canal. It's probably nothing, but when we were at St Malo, the ship coming under fire and gybing suddenly, I glimpsed a strange-looking vessel moored in a wet dock. I took note of all the ships I saw, and wrote it down as 'large open boat', but what you said about the canal just now has got me thinking."

"What did it look like?"

"Well, I only saw it for a moment, but it had very square ends, straight sides, and inside it I got the impression that there were rows of thwarts, so that there could be, I don't know how many, but a lot of rowers and room for people to sit. A lot of people."

Snowden began to understand what he was saying. "You mean, like an invasion barge?"

"Well, not exactly a barge. It had quite a bit of sheer, but, well, it looked as though it might have been intended to fit exactly in a lock."

Suddenly, Snowden felt very sober.

The preparations had been thorough, and Morlaix knew that Bonaparte's visit had gone well. The barges had manoeuvred on the Etang de Bétineuc without any collisions, and had then been run up onto the beach, with the men jumping out enthusiastically, wading ashore, and forming up in good order. At first, Bonaparte was on his horse alongside Murat and Talleyrand, but being the man he was, had soon decided to try the experience of landing from a barge himself, and had ended up waist deep in muddy water. Murat had thrown himself enthusiastically into the activity, but Talleyrand had remained resolutely on his horse, with the dignity befitting a cardinal.

There was a dinner that night in the great boat-building shed, amidst the mass of partly constructed barges, cordage, oars and piles of equipment. Bonaparte was in ebullient mood, rising to speak in praise of Morlaix and the others involved in the project, especially Bisset, whose face glowed with the approbation from Napoléon, as well it might, and declaring a week's holiday for the workmen.

Afterwards, Bonaparte, Murat and Morlaix sat round the dining table in Morlaix's house, while Talleyrand talked to Dominique. "You have done a fine job, Breton."

"Thank you, but there is still work to be done."

"We think that there is much that you could teach the people at Boulogne," interjected Murat, his splendid uniform glittering. "We would like you to accompany us when we go there tomorrow to inspect their preparations. I have instructed Colonel Greffier to have the soldiers ready for six o'clock in the morning."

Morlaix had expected that Bonaparte might ask him to go to Boulogne, and had made arrangements for Dominique to return to Paris, but that they were intending to take the soldiers with them was shocking. "Sir," he replied, addressing Bonaparte, "if you take the soldiers, this place will be unguarded."

"What are you worried about? I believe the Chouans have been brought to heel."

"They may have been, but the English?"

"You are in France, Breton, in the middle of Brittany. The English know we are at Boulogne, but they don't know about this place, and besides, it is miles from the sea."

"I know, sir, but we have always taken great precautions to guard the place, and the English are alert. There was an English ship, in the roadstead of St Malo. I could not have found my way into the place in the way she did, like a Malouine fisherman. She was there simply to reconnoitre, and I believe there was an admiral on board. An admiral aboard a ship that size! I believe it was Admiral Sausmarez, the man in charge of their *Channel Islands* station."

Morlaix gave the English name for the Islands, as though to emphasise the nearness of the enemy.

"Sir, I know what you said about the Chouans is true, but some *Bretons*," he emphasised the word, "are still not entirely enthusiastic about the republic, and it is not far to the Normandes."

"You worry too much. I need the men, Breton. You have trained them well in their work, their confidence and morale are high, and they will be able to show their comrades in the *Armée d'Angleterre* how it is done. Before long they will return, but in the interval the chance of the English doing any harm is remote."

Talleyrand moved over. Ever the politician, he saw how the land was lying and pitched in to support Bonaparte. "Morlaix, what you have said is true, but we do need you and the men you have trained. The operation at Boulogne is on a grand scale, but it is nowhere near what you have here in terms of training and efficiency. If we cannot use the Armée d'Angleterre soon, we will lose our opportunity. We need you and the men there, quickly."

Morlaix saw that further debate was useless, and made his excuses and left the room. As he was putting his coat on, Dominique came into the hall. "Where are you going, father? It's raining outside."

"I am going to visit Lieutenant Maydieu." Maydieu was Morlaix's assistant, in charge of the naval contingent which manned the barges.

"Why Maydieu? Can it not wait until tomorrow? He will be in bed."

Morlaix leaned his head close to his daughter. "It cannot wait, Dominique. Our leader is taking the soldiers to Boulogne. It may be a terrible mistake because it leaves the base here undefended. If the English come, and God knows they have friends enough around here, Maydieu and his men will be all that there is."

Dominique started to protest.

"Dominique, tomorrow you must start for Paris. Take Madame Peress. I will ask Maydieu to provide an officer to accompany you. Now, go back and keep Talleyrand amused."

Snowden and Jack, with *Clementine*'s commander, Scoresby, sat together in front of Sausmarez's desk, facing the admiral, with his secretary to one side. Scoresby, who had been quick to appreciate Jack's assessment of the French plans, spoke first, rather nervously Snowden thought, a man more at home on the quarterdeck than in the admiral's study.

"Your honour, Lieutenant Snowden and Midshipman Stone have some intelligence which I believe is of the first importance, and I ask your indulgence and believe it might be appropriate if Mr Stone ...." His voice rather trailed off.

Sausmarez looked at Jack. "Mr Stone."

"Thank you, your honour." Jack's nervousness and diffidence were a thing of the past. His voice was firm, self-assured, confident.   "When we were in the foretop, sir, that is, *Clementine*'s foretop at St Malo, just as the French fired on us and we gybed her round ...."

"I remember it well, Mr Stone."

"So do I," interjected Scoresby. "Damned hot work for a few minutes."

"Indeed, Mr Scoresby."

"Sorry, sir."

Jack continued. "Well, sir, I noted this down, but as she gybed, and there was a lot of smoke, and the men were setting the topsails, so it was difficult to see ...."

"It was, I was on my way down by then," reminisced Sausmarez.

"Well, sir, as I said, it was difficult to see, and we were moving fast, but I just glimpsed a large boat, a barge, sort of, rather a strange-looking one. I, well ...." Jack was trying to avoid telling Sausmarez that he had told the First Lieutenant about the barge when he had handed in his tally of ships in the harbour, so carried on. "Last night, I was thinking about it. I've made a sketch of the barge, sir. Here it is." He pushed a sheet of paper across the table. Sausmarez picked it up, and the secretary half stood up to look for himself.

"It's the best I can do, sir. I only saw the barge, if that is what it was, briefly. The thing was about sixty feet long, pretty square at the ends, raised bow. There was a lot of smoke about, but I think, in fact I'm pretty sure, that there were a large number of thwarts inside the hull and there were certainly a quantity of oar openings in her sides."

Sausmarez nodded.

"I think, sir, that this barge is intended to carry a large number of men."

"Do you, Mr Stone?"

Snowden felt he could hardly contain himself, and interjected. "Sir, you remember that we went to Paris. Well, we set out from Maloes. We went up the Rance by boat, and at Dinan they were building a lock, a canal lock, you know."

Sausmarez nodded.

"Sir, they were changing the river into a canal – a canal like the Royal Canal in the south, from Toulouse to the Med, and the ones they're building in Manchester."

Sausmarez's eyes narrowed in concentration.

"We followed the canal on horseback, just to have a look at it. It is going to Rennes, and I think it will eventually go to the Biscay coast."

Snowden, bursting with excitement, stood up abruptly and walked to a large map of France on the wall. "See here, sir, the Ille and then the Vilaine rivers. St Malo to Rennes, Rennes to Redon. Channel to Biscay. But here's the thing, sir, which Mr Stone has figured out, God bless his soul. At a place called Bétineuc, on the canal, we saw they were building sheds, huge sheds, with forges and sawpits, and things like that, and there were piles of timber, and slipways. It was obvious that they were intending to build barges."

Jack continued, "We didn't think much of it at the time, sir, but we did remark that they must be intending to build a prodigious quantity of barges for the canal. And there was another thing that we didn't think too much of, but there was a lake, quite large, twenty acres perhaps, with a sandy beach. I think the lake may have been made, or enlarged. An artificial pond, sir."

Sausmarez nodded. "Please continue, Mr Stone."

"As I said, sir, the barge I saw in St Malo seemed to be intended to carry men, soldiers. I don't know why it was there, practising in the sea perhaps, but I think it was designed to fit exactly in the locks on the canal. Fulton showed me pictures of the barges they use on the Royal Canal, and that's what it was like, except it had more sheer and looked more seamanlike, if you know what I mean. Sir, I consider that the French are building barges at Bétineuc, using the lake there to practise, and when they're ready, probably when there's a settled spell, sir, they'll load soldiers onto the barges at Bétineuc, all equipped, go down the canal to the Rance and then into the Channel, and while we're watching them at Boulogne, they'll be on the English side in a day or so."

"There were certainly a number of French men o' war at Maloes," said Sausmarez, "more than I'd expected. I wondered what they intended with them."

"And that's not all, sir," said Snowden.

"Indeed, Mr Snowden?"

"No, sir. When we were at Paris, we were invited to a very grand soiree. It turned out that it was at the house of Captain Morlaix – you know, sir, the man that led their Weymouth expedition."

"Yes," said Sausmarez, "I have heard of Morlaix. That was certainly a coincidence, Stone. Morlaix is an extraordinary man I believe."

"Well, Mr Stone was talking to Morlaix's daughter, and Fouché was watching them."

Sausmarez's surprise was visible. "Damn – talking to Morlaix's daughter were you, Stone? And Fouché, how did you know it was Fouché?"

Snowden smiled. The winning card. "Well, sir, Talleyrand told me. I was playing at cards with him. Losing badly."

"Playing at cards with Talleyrand. Upon my word, Mr Snowden, I don't doubt you were losing."

Jack spoke again. "Sir, Dominique, I mean Mademoiselle Morlaix, told me that she was about to go to Brittany with her father, who was to take charge of a large project."

"Did she now?" said Sausmarez.

Snowden spoke again. "Talleyrand warned us to clear out, sharpish. Apparently Fouché took a very dim view of Mr Stone's recent activities in France, and, well, Mr Stone was not strictly on the books at the time, so to speak. Talleyrand reminded me of Captain Smith's misadventures, so we were on our way out of Paris directly. Hardly stopped until we were at Havre."

Sausmarez was silent for what seemed like a long time.

"My word, gentlemen, I hardly know where to begin. If I had not known both of you for some time I would scarce have believed it, but if Boney could build a fleet in the middle of France, and train it well away from us, and then sail straight across the Channel, well, he might get away with it. I expect he'd pay us a visit here as well, on his way. Morlaix's well in with Boney, you saw that in Paris, and he wouldn't be wasted on anything trifling. If he's in charge it will be a pretty serious endeavour."

He's gone for it, thought Snowden. I hope to God we're right.

"Damn, Stone, Snowden, I think you may be right. But the question is, what should we do about it?"

Sausmarez studied the map on the wall, feeling apart from the everyday sounds of his house and the street outside, as life continued around him. He felt the irony of his present situation, simultaneously at home and commander of the naval squadron defending the Channel Islands.

Napoléon had to invade and defeat Britain. Sausmarez doubted that he would be able to do it from Boulogne, which was closely guarded by the Royal Navy, and he was reasonably sure that any expedition mounted from Brest or Rochefort would have severe difficulty in evading the British blockade. French expeditions to Ireland had not finished well, defeated by the weather and unpractised crews as much as the British navy.

He had always thought that St Malo, with the Channel Islands as a stepping-stone, was a possibility. It would be a sharp chance, but he had been at the Nile and knew that Bonaparte was not frightened of risk. That was why Sausmarez had fought the political battle to strengthen his Channel Islands' Squadron, and why he had taken *Clementine* into St Malo to reconnoitre. Though reassured by the lack of invasion barges, he had wondered at the number of French naval ships in the harbour, and surprised by the obvious readiness and efficiency of the garrison. There was something going on there, without doubt, and this is what had made him think that the theory advanced by the young men was plausible.

He surmised that the memory of the English "descent" on St Malo in 1758, led by Marlborough, which had resulted in the loss of hundreds of French ships, might make the French wary of keeping invasion barges in St Malo.

Morlaix's involvement was worrying. He was known in the Royal Navy as a skilful, determined and resourceful commander, the man who had amazed the world by almost kidnapping the King from the front at Weymouth. Stone and Snowden's description of Morlaix's obvious proximity to the centre of power in Paris, underlined by the importance of the guests at the soiree at his house – Talleyrand, Fouché – made Sausmarez think that if he really was involved in an invasion scheme, it should be taken seriously.

He called for his secretary. "A despatch for the Admiralty."

"Very well, Sir James."

When the despatch was complete, and the clerk had gone out to organise a fast packet to take it to Portsmouth, which had good communications with London, Sausmarez thought of the times involved. Probably two days to London, at least a day or so of consideration, and then issuing orders, readying of ships. It would be a long time before anything was done. Too long? Those warships in St Malo, the crack garrison. Could Morlaix organise and exercise an invasion force so far from the sea, and get it out into the Channel in good order? And if he could, how advanced were his plans?

Sausmarez did not know the answer to these questions, but he knew if Morlaix could get his barges to sea in good order, with a strong escort, that the Channel Islands and then England herself would be at risk.

He went outside into the square and looked up at the sky. The wind was light, the weather settled. His duty lay clear before him. He had to find out what was going on at Bétineuc, and quickly, but first he had a vist to make.

He called for his horse.

Sausmarez pulled up his horse near the cottage inhabited by Trezeguet, and hitched it and the one he had been leading to a gate. Trezeguet was a Chouan rebel who he had rescued from a beach when the Quiberon rebellion had gone so disastrously wrong. That had been some time ago, and since then the man had been living quietly in Guernsey, making a living by growing and selling vegetables. Sausmarez knew that from time to time people and goods travelled between Guernsey and Brittany, despite the blockade.

He walked to the cottage, and a woman came to the door at his knock. He had obviously disturbed a meal, as he could see into a small room where a man had paused in eating to look towards the door.

Sausmarez spoke, in Guernsey patios. "I would like to speak to Monsieur Trezeguet."

The woman beckoned him into the room and the man at the table rose.

"Monsieur Trezeguet, good afternoon. I apologise for interrupting your meal."

"Sir James, I have so much to thank you for that the interruption of a meal is trivial. How may I help? Please, let us come out, into the garden."

Sausmarez glanced at the woman, busying herself inside, as he stood with Trezeguet in the garden, the insects humming round them.

"Have you heard of a canal that is being built between Dinan and Rennes? A canal for barges?"

Trezeguet looked surprised by the question, but answered confidently. "Yes, sir, I have certainly heard of this canal. The works are very great, and many people are employed."

"Do you know how close it is to completion?"

"No, sir, but I have heard that the effort is considerable. It is said that when it is complete it will bring a great improvement in trade to the area." He looked at Sausmarez questioningly.

"Monsieur Trezeguet, I appreciate that it may be inconvenient, but I would like you to accompany me to St Pierre, immediately. I have a horse for you."

Snowden counted nine men around the admiral's table that evening at his town house in St Peter's. Sausmarez sat opposite him, flanked by Peterson of *Invincible*, the squadron's flagship, and the admiral's secretary, Masters. On Snowden's side of the table sat Captain Wain of the marines, Scoresby, *Clementine*'s commander, Jack, the admiral's pilot, Jean Breton, and Trezeguet, the Chouan rebel.

Sausmarez looked at the men round the table. "Gentlemen, I have asked you here so that you may hear the outline of a plan that has been devised by myself and Captain Wain. It is a plan that involves considerable risk, but the stakes are so high that I believe that the risks are justified. Gentlemen, we must act with expedition, and in complete secrecy."

Snowden felt a thrill of excitement.

"Mr Masters, if you please."

Masters stood and went to the huge map of France on the wall. "We believe that it is possible that the enemy is building a base for the invasion of England at a place called Bétineuc." Masters pointed Bétineuc out on the map. There was a murmur from the assembled men. Snowden nudged Jack.

"The reason that the French can build a base here, so far from the sea, is that they are building a canal from Dinard ...." Masters pointed at the map again.

Sausmarez took up the speech: "Thank you, Masters. ... to Rennes. We believe in time the canal will reach Redon, connecting the Channel with Biscay. At this place, Bétineuc, we have reason to believe that the enemy has the capacity to build a quantity of barges, and to exercise them on a lake which he has built or enlarged for that purpose. At our recent excursion to Maloes in *Clementine*, we saw a large boat, which we believe is a barge designed for this purpose, and we further believe that the project is in the charge of one Captain Morlaix, who is both powerfully connected at the highest levels in France and a very capable commander. Our intention is to reconnoitre this putative base. It is unlikely that we will be able to do it any damage, but if we know it is there, we will be able to prepare, and much of its power will be dissipated because of that."

He looked round the room. "Simply put, gentlemen, our intention is to embark a party led by Captain Wain into boats, somewhere off St Cas ...."

He paused while Masters pointed this out on the map. There was a stir in the room.

"Yes, gentlemen, I know that the place does not have happy memories for the Navy, or the Army for that matter, but we are not making a *descent* as such, but merely a light reconnaissance."

Snowden knew that Sausmarez was referring to 1758, when a British expedition against St Malo had turned into a disastrous rout as soldiers attempted to evacuate from the beach at St Cas.

Sausmarez continued, "… and then enter the River Arguenon with the tide under the boats, and to make as far inland as possible before leaving the boats and proceeding on foot quickly, very quickly, to Bétineuc. It will be a hard march, but it should be possible to arrive there before dawn. Mr Trezeguet has agreed to guide us, and Mr Snowden will take charge of the naval arrangements. Both Mr Snowden and Mr Stone will accompany the party, as they have been to Bétineuc before. Once the party has come to a conclusion about what is going on, it will return to the north, to the boats. Because of the nature of the task, which will involve very swift travel by foot, only young and fit men will be taken. The tide serves in four days, the thirteenth, and you'll have a bit of moon by about two."

Sausmarez paused and looked round the room. Scoresby put his hand up.

"Sir, what is the feeling of the population thereabouts?"

"I believe that the people there are still rather unenthusiastic about the Republic, but probably they cannot be relied upon. Monsieur Trezeguet will canvass what support he can, but safety is in expedition, gentlemen. Speed is of the essence."

Snowden looked at Jack, who did not appear to be particularly enthusiastic at the prospect of action.

Snowden had a thought, and spoke. "Sir, will there be anything by way of diversion?"

"Indeed there will, Mr Snowden."

The men stood up to leave, but Sausmarez held up his hand.

"I need hardly add that secrecy is vital. Everything must be done on a most confidential basis. Tomorrow morning you will put yourselves at the disposal of Captain Wain, who assures me that you and the men will be exercised most relentlessly. Do you have anything to add, Captain Wain?"

"I do, Sir James. We will commence our exercises tonight at eight o'clock."

Chapter 15 – Preparation

Snowden felt tired beyond belief as he laid himself down in *Demoiselle*'s cabin. When had they started? Probably about six last night, and they had only just finished. He had gone back to his ship, asked for eight volunteers from the sailors, and then returned with two of the French ship's boats to the town.

Captain Wain was indeed relentless. Jack had taken charge of one boat and Snowden had the other. They had taken them to the town and loaded the marines. There were too few sailors to completely man the oars, so they had spent a frustrating hour just off the land, teaching the marines to row properly.

And then in the gathering evening they had practised landing and hauling the boats up onto the land, stopping briefly for bread and cheese, until it was dark, and then Wain had led them out onto the Island's lanes, setting a brisk pace. Wain experimented with different techniques, eventually settling on a hundred paces trotting and then another hundred walking. By the time dawn broke they were exhausted, but they had covered miles, and they were starting to become confident in the dark.

Snowden groaned. There was another four days of this.

Clementine idled, hove to, just off the coast at St Cast, the silhouette of the land just visible off the starboard bow. She was as far into the estuary of the Arguenon as Scoresby, advised by Jean Breton, had cared to take her, and indeed she had bumped once or twice already. The saving grace was the rising tide.

Snowden, with Stone, Captain Wain of the marines and Scoresby, stood on the poop, looking towards St Malo, a few miles to the west. The night was dark and the only light on the ship was from the dimly illuminated binnacle. The two boats were alongside, with the landing party already embarked, and from time to time the men on the poop could hear the boats bump softly against the side of the ship.

"Any moment now," said Scoresby to Snowden, and as he spoke the sky to the west was illuminated by the red glow of rocket trails, followed by flashes from muzzles of guns and from explosions as the rockets landed.

"That'll get their attention," said Snowden, and they walked across the deck to board the boats, accompanied by the sound of distant explosions.

In the dark, the boats set off up the river, the men pulling strongly on the muffled oars, their progress made swift by the tide flooding under them. Snowden, at the helm of the leading boat, strained his eyes into the darkness ahead and to the sides, where the banks were just visible in a blacker line of darkness against the sky. He could hear, just astern, the oar splashes of the second boat, and occasionally a quiet order, "Easy now" or "Give way there," from Jack at the helm. Both boats had dim blue lights already lit and burning under cover, ready to display if they became separated, but darkness was their ally, and they hoped to avoid any lights if they could.

The show from St Malo continued, and Snowden realised that the distraction, which was indeed on a grand scale, had the unintended consequence of potentially silhouetting them against it to any spectators on the shore. Snowden hoped that there were no such spectators, and perhaps there were not, as the land was desolate, and no doubt sparsely inhabited.

The channel gradually narrowed, and the men occasionally cursed as their oars struck bottom. Snowden, at the tiller, felt Trezeguet pull at his sleeve and heard him whisper, "Village."

Snowden remembered that there was a village on the map, and ordered in a soft voice, "Easy oar." The boat slowed, the men glad of the breather.

He heard, from close behind him, an oath, and then Jack's quiet voice, calm and clear, "Backwater together" and then "Hold water," followed by "Give way. Easy oar."

The boats crept past the village, more sensed than seen, and when it seemed they were past, pulled strongly away upriver, the tide still carrying them. They passed close to a dimly seen house on a bend in the river, and were startled by the barking of a dog, followed by a voice crying out loudly in enquiry. Discovered, thought Snowden, it was bound to happen.

"Keep quiet," he ordered in an undertone to the men, but was startled when Trezeguet let out a screeching sound, like an owl in a wood. To Snowden's amazement, a few seconds later, an answering owl call was heard from the bank, and the dog abruptly stopped barking.

"We still have some friends here," the Chouan whispered in Snowden's ear.

"I'm very glad to hear it."

Half an hour later, it was becoming clear that they could not go much further, especially as the tides were getting smaller and there would be less water when they returned from their reconnaissance. They could just make out a wood on the right bank of the river, and Snowden turned and whistled softly twice, giving the signal for Jack's boat to come alongside.

"Welcome to France, Mr Stone," said Snowden, speaking to a dimly made out Jack.

"Thank you, Lieutenant Snowden."

"I think we'll put the boats ashore here. There's quite a large village ahead, and we don't really want to get involved in that."

"Very well."

"We'll put a cable's length or so between the boats in the woods, so that if one is discovered, perhaps the other one may not be." It was a stretch to believe that, but it was worth a try.

Snowden steered his boat into the shore, and, accompanied by a great deal of heartfelt but subdued cursing, they were dragged a good way from the shoreline, into a scrubby wood, turned over with the oars underneath, and covered in loose branches.

The men sat on the boats, recovering, eating their sparse meal which was enlivened by distant explosions from the direction of St Malo.

Snowden turned to Captain Wain, who was sitting next to him. "Well, Captain Wain, the naval part of the expedition appears to be at an end for now, and I put myself and my men at your disposal."

"Thank you, Lieutenant Snowden. We will proceed as planned."

Trezeguet, who had gone off into the woods while the Englishmen were dealing with the boats, returned and indicated that there was a road, or what passed for a road in Brittany, nearby.

Snowden grudgingly admitted to himself that the hard work Wain had put them through in Guernsey was paying off, as the men made their way quietly though the woods and formed up silently on the road. Wain, at the head of the column with Trezeguet, whistled softly and they set off southward, two abreast, alternately trotting and walking, the sailors in the middle, marines ahead and behind them, each man carrying a musket.

Chapter 17 – Diversion

The squadron had arrived off St Malo as the sun was setting. Sausmarez, aboard his flagship, the 74-gun *Invincible*, knew the presence of the squadron would be noticed ashore and that the defences would be in a state of high readiness. The squadron consisted of five ships – *Invincible*, the bomb vessel *Terror*, the frigate *Hera* and two schooners, *Clementine* and *Provident*. There was considerable activity on board as the officers took bearings of known landmarks ashore so as to establish their ships' positions.

As darkness fell, the ships sailed in line ahead along the main channel leading into the port, each showing a dim blue light astern to guide the ship behind her. The line was led by *Iolanthe*, piloted by her studious commander Lieutenant Rigby. On *Invincible*'s quarterdeck, several officers peered into the gloom, attempting to identify the dark outlines of land which were just visible against the slightly paler sky, and if possible to take compass bearings of them and to transfer them to the charts which were laid out on a table in the cabin.

Invincible's commander and Sausmarez's flag captain, Peterson, said in a matter-of-fact voice, "Passed Cézembre, sir. *Hera* will be anchoring about now."

They listened intently but could hear no sound of the frigate ahead taking in sail or dropping her anchors. She would have to lay a kedge anchor out in a boat, so that the ship could be oriented for maximum effectiveness.

"Delicate work, Peterson."

"It is, sir."

A few minutes passed. Sausmarez thought that his reputation, built up over the years, and which had left him loaded with honours, could be brought to nothing tonight by the slightest error in navigation. A ship going aground just off the French coast did not bear thinking about.

"Bomb will be anchoring now, sir."

"Thank you, Peterson." The bomb, *Terror*, was to anchor at a distance from the town equivalent to the extreme range of her mortars.

The minutes dragged on. Sausmarez heard an officer say, "Three minutes if you please, sir."

Peterson replied, "Very well" and then "The kedge, Mr Hartnell, and take in sail."

There was a running of men and a splash as the kedge anchor was let go from the stern. Men worked at braces and sheets, and others in the rigging gathered up the main and foretopsails. The ship, carrying her way, forged slowly ahead.

"Three cables gone, sir," said an unseen officer, meaning that six hundred yards of anchor cables had been paid out since the kedge anchor was dropped.

"Snub her then."

Peterson, staring intently at the dimly lit compass, said, "Best bower now, she's nicely lined up." There was a splash as the best bower anchor was released from the bow.

"Heave in on the kedge warp. One and a half cables. Keep some strain on the bower warp, let the anchor dig in." Sausmarez could hear the pawls of the windless clacking as the cables were adjusted.

An unseen officer called, "She's there now, sir."

Peterson bent over the binnacle again, and then peered intently to port through the darkness. He dropped to his knees. "I can see it, just where it should be," referring to the fort on Petit Bey island.

Peterson joined Sausmarez on the quarterdeck. "We seem to be in good order, Sir James."

"I congratulate you, Captain Peterson. Let us hope that all the ships are conducted in a similarly efficient manner."

"Thank you, Sir James, I'm sure they will be. It wants ten minutes of nine."

They could detect little activity in the fort. Probably the people in it could not see the great ship anchored a quarter of a mile away, the guns of her terrible broadside pointed directly at them.

Sausmarez could feel a supressed excitement gripping the ship as the minutes ticked by.

"Nine o'clock, Sir James," said Peterson, conversationally.

"Carry on, Captain Peterson."

"Very well, Sir James," and then, louder, "Fire at will."

Invincible's port broadside roared out, one gun at a time, deafening in the calm night, the muzzle flashes a blinding, vivid orange, illuminating, briefly, their target, the Petit Bey fort. Overhead, he saw, but did not hear, the red trails of the Congreve rockets launched from the bomb ship, high over *Invincible*, and then saw the flashes from explosions as they landed beyond the town, to where they hoped the naval ships were berthed. He heard the flat "crumps" as *Terror*'s mortars fired, and a few seconds later, rather subdued explosions.

"Short, I reckon, in the sea," said Peterson, referring to the likely destination of the mortar shells, and then grabbed the taffrail as *Invincible*'s broadside roared out again. Far off, to seaward, they heard *Hera*'s smaller broadside unleashed against the Cézembre fort.

A fire started ashore, and by its light, they could clearly make out the ramparts of the main fort.

"That'll give 'em something to aim at," said Peterson, and the bombardment continued, with more fires starting.

Before long, the Petit Bey fort began to fire back at *Invincible*, presumably aiming at the muzzle flashes. Balls screamed overhead, and some struck the sides of the ship, but did little damage. It was notoriously difficult for a wooden ship to subdue a stone fort, especially as aiming from a moving warship was more difficult than from a stationary land base, but as *Invincible*'s broadsides crashed out, the fort's fire grew desultory and then stopped altogether.

"Interesting to see what it looks like in the morning," said Peterson, during a pause in the firing, as a delicate combination of touches on sails and anchors turned the ship so that the guns could bear on the second fort, Grand Bey.

"Probably just keeping their heads down," replied Sausmarez.

By one o'clock, *Invincible* was firing at the town, where several fires were burning as a result of *Terror*'s bombardment. *Invincible* had been turned end for end, so that her starboard battery was active, and she was now pointed towards the open sea.

A pale sliver of moon was becoming visible, and Sausmarez spoke to Peterson. "The green rocket now, if you please."

The rocket sizzled into the air, and a few minutes later the pale shadow of a ship slid past, heading along the channel into the town. They could just make out the boats she was towing.

"There's *Provident* now," said Sausmarez to Peterson, in an interval between broadsides, indicating the silent ship. "God help them."

Twenty minutes or so later, a rather bedraggled man stood on *Invincible*'s quarterdeck in front of Sausmarez and Peterson. The 74's guns continued to fire, but more slowly, the expenditure of shot and powder more difficult to justify now that the need for the diversion had, they hoped, become less acute.

Sausmarez looked at the man in front of him. "Lieutenant Jameson, how fares *Provident*?"

"We left her, sir, sailing close hauled, fore staysails and mainsail only. Nicely balanced, she's practically sailing herself. Lieutenant Randall took the helm, and ordered us into the boat."

"Did he now?"

"Yes, sir, I know that wasn't the plan, but he was in no mood to argue."

"I'm sure he wasn't."

"The fires are lit, sir. It's only a matter of twenty minutes or so, though it's anybody's guess really, before she really goes up. Poor old ship."

"Never mind the ship. What boats does he have?"

"The jollyboat, sir, but she's a heavy thing. He's got another boat as well. He got it in Guernsey, a little flat-bottomed little thing, apparently came from a Grand Banks schooner, or something."

"Thank you, Jameson, your commander is setting a brave example. Let us hope he does not leave it too late."

Since he was a boy, Randall had always wondered what it would be like to sail a ship by himself, singlehanded, with no crew. Well, he knew now, and the main feeling he had was one of loneliness. He had nothing to do except steer, and the crew had balanced the ship so well before their departure that he hardly had to do that, only to give her an occasional spoke now and then as she bore up when there was a puff of wind, and even then, he thought, left to her own devices, she would probably have come back on course anyway.

The first lieutenant, Jameson, had urged him strongly, in an urgent whisper, to leave the ship as they had planned. "Damnation, man, do you mean to get yourself killed? The ship will do her duty without you."

But in the end Jameson had obeyed his orders, and had taken himself and the few members of the crew remaining on board off into the longboat. Randall had known that the ship couldn't be trusted to find her way without anyone at the helm. He was twenty-one years old, but he had been in the Navy since he was twelve. He was from a naval family, as well, and had been raised, as everybody in a naval was, on tales of Drake. He knew the opprobrium that had been heaped on the unlucky, or perhaps feeble, commanders of the fireships Drake had sent against the Armada at Gravelines, and he was not about to let that happen to him. No, *Provident* needed a pilot, he was her commander, and it had to be him. He had the little dory ready, and knew which way to row her, and he was damned well going to see the thing through. He shivered in the wind spilled by the mainsail, and made minute adjustments to the lashing on the helm. It was lonely, though.

Provident was well into the roadstead now, the town open before him on the port bow. He could see the flames starting to escape from the hold. Not long now.

Long minutes passed, and he saw ahead, beyond the town, a mass of ships' masts against the sky. That was it. If he could get *Provident* in among them. He adjusted the lashing on the helm, and wiped his eyes clear of the sweat running down his brow. The heat of the flames was becoming intense, but the ship was steering well now, straight for the moored French men o' war, though they were difficult to see beyond the flames raging above the deck.

Just a minute longer.

He heard a noise behind him, and looked to see a man, dressed in the most fantastic uniform, topped off by a tall shako, climb over the port rail, jump down nimbly onto the deck, and then run towards him, brandishing what looked like a cavalry sabre in his hand. He realised immediately that the man was boarding from a boat, unseen in the darkness beyond the fires. The man was by himself, but Randall was sure that more would follow.

"Time to go, Randall," he thought to himself. He glanced down at the wheel, saw it was lashed, pulled the pistols from his belt, fired them in the direction of the advancing man, and then ran to the starboard rail, slashed through the painter of the dory with his cutlass, and dived overboard.

The cold of the water was a shock after the heat of the fires aboard *Provident*, but he felt a great sense of relief as his head emerged above the surface and he saw his dory, floating free nearby, its shape starkly silhouetted by light from the burning ship. Relief turned momentarily to horror when he thought that the light dory would be blown by the wind faster than he could swim.

He trod water, forcing himself to calm down as he methodically removed his jacket, and then he set off after the dory, sometimes gaining on it, but losing ground when the wind piped up. He was almost at his last extremity, and close enough to the land that he could see and hear people ashore, when his foot unexpectedly touched something underwater. He instinctively recoiled, but immediately realised that he had felt the painter, trailing just under the water.

With the last of his strength, he redoubled his efforts, and was rewarded when he felt his hand touch the rope. He grasped it firmly, and hauled himself along it until he was at the bow of the dinghy. He hauled himself up as far as he could on the painter, grabbed the gunwhale with one hand, and went hand over hand along it, gripping the rope in his mouth, until he was at the dory's stern. The land was so close now that he could hear the small waves of the harbour breaking on the shore. He heard a shout from the land, whether it was directed at him he did not know, but with the last of his strength he flicked the painter into the slot in the stern for a sculling oar, and heaved himself aboard. For a moment he lay on the bottom boards, but there was another shout, and sat on the thwart, shipped the oars and started to row towards the sea.

He looked over his shoulder and saw the *Provident*, now a mass of fire, apparently ashore on the west bank of the Rance, her guns, which they had loaded before starting out, firing as they were heated, or sparks found their way into their powder charges. The Frenchmen must have been able to turn her away from the intended target. He had not got the fireship amongst the frigates, but he thought that Drake would have approved of his efforts. As he watched, the blazing mainmast with its sails on fire collapsed in a shower of sparks, and he found himself hoping that the boarders had escaped.

The tide was against him, but the wind was reasonably fair, and he managed to keep away from the town, where fires were burning. He could see figures running and a chain of men in uniform passing buckets of water from the sea to a burning building, urged on by a dumpy figure on a huge white horse.

He could see *Invincible* in the distance, occasionally starkly lit by the muzzle flashes of her thirty-two pounders. Though the ship was firing away from him as he approached, the noise was deafening, and he had to hail several times before he was heard, and had no further recollection of events, apart from an impression of being lifted by strong hands, until he found himself sitting on a chair in the cabin, covered in a blanket, with Peterson and Sausmarez standing in front of him.

"Well done, my boy," said Sausmarez.

Randall looked at him. "I didn't get among the frigates, there were boarders, a man in an astonishing uniform. I jumped, and they must have got her round so she was heading away from them."

A servant came in and handed glasses to the three men. Sausmarez looked at Randall and raised his glass. "Your health, Lieutenant Randall. You have done your duty."

They drank. Sausmarez put down his glass and turned towards the door, the marine sentry standing aside to let him pass.

Randall said, in a voice perhaps not as steady as he would have liked, "Sir, Boney's there, I saw him, on a white horse, plain as you like."

The pace of the march was relentless: one hundred paces trotting, a hundred paces walking, the pattern set by Wain at the head of the column. Snowden marched at Wain's right and Trezeguet on his left. It was almost pitch dark, but there was enough of a moon to see the road, rough as it was, in front of them, and the dark hedges on either side. From time to time Trezeguet would pull Wain's sleeve, and the column would slow down as they passed a cottage or farm. Once they passed through a small village and were challenged by a sleepy shout, but Trezeguet let out one of his unearthly owl screeches and the voice was immediately silenced.

When they stopped for water – "Five minutes only" was the message from Wain, passed back along the column – the men sat on the verge, and Snowden walked back to speak to Jack.

"How are you enjoying Navy life?" he asked in jest.

"Having second thoughts," replied Jack. Snowden was not entirely sure he was joking.

They could just make out the card of the small compass that Snowden carried, and it confirmed that they were heading south.

"Nice to be back in France, though," said Snowden.

Jack did not answer, and Snowden decided that he was perhaps not in the mood for jocularity.

They resumed the march, from time to time pausing at crossroads while Trezeguet thought, often for a disquietingly long time, about which road they should take. Snowden could tell from the stars, however, that they were generally heading south.

The march was not something that Snowden felt he would soon forget. With every step they took they were further from the coast and the familiar and secure "wooden world" of the Navy. He felt unease that they were entirely in the hands of the Chouan, and could only imagine the reward Trezeguet might reap if he betrayed them to the French. He kept a close watch on the Breton, and from time to time touched the hilt of his cutlass.

The march went on, exhaustingly, for several hours. At times there would come the sound of a fall, followed by muffled cursing, as one of the men tripped unseeingly on the uneven surface and sometimes brought some of the following men down with him.

After this had happened for the fourth time, Trezeguet whispered to Wain, "We have made good progress, Captain. I believe it would be better if we slowed so that we made less noise."

Wain nodded agreement. He turned to the sergeant behind him. "Pass back: approaching destination. Quiet."

Suddenly, without warning, they came upon a river in the dim moonlight. There were no trees beside it, and the earth along the bank was disturbed.

"Halt," said Wain to the sergeant, unnecessarily, as he and the column had already stopped. Wain ordered the men to lie on the ground, and passed back for Jack to come to the head of the column.

Jack and Snowden walked away from the column for a few paces, and put their heads close together.

"This is the canal, Percy."

"I'm sure you're right."

"It seems pretty straight here, and there's that church steeple over there. I think it looks familiar."

"It does to me as well, but its damnably difficult to see."

Snowden looked up at the stars. "Couple of hours to dawn, I reckon. I think we stopped for a bite to eat just down there, in the good old days."

"I think so as well, Perce," said Jack, "and they do seem like very good days now, don't they?"

"Cheer up, my boy. Soon be back in the Navy. Look, Jack, I think the lake is over there." He pointed with his outstretched arm. "Perhaps a mile away."

"I think so too. We sat a couple of cables further along, and had our bit of food."

"So, if we walk along the canal, that way, we'll …"

"Run into half the French army, most like," said Jack gloomily.

"Come on, buck up, man."

"Sorry, Perce, I'll make an effort."

They walked back together and spoke to Wain and Trezeguet, who were relieved that they had arrived at the right place.

Wain whispered, "That hill over there, well wooded. If we made our way up it, would we be able to see the place when it gets light?"

Snowden thought about it, trying desperately to reconcile his memory of a happy, sunny day in peacetime with the current dark reality.

"I reckon there's a good chance. What do you think, Jack?"

"I agree. I think I remember that hill. I think there's a sort of monument thing on it, but it should give a good view."

The column made its way, as quietly as it could, over the relatively open country near the river and through the dimly seen wood. It wasn't much of a hill, but the land around was flat, and when they got to the top they could just make out, very close, the canal and the buildings of the French establishment, with the gleam of the lake visible just beyond.

Wain set pickets, and the men sat down, eating. Snowden realised, with sudden clarity, that it did not matter, strategically, if they were discovered. If the French noticed them, their very presence near the base would mean that its value was much depreciated, as the element of surprise would be gone. He had no doubt that Sausmarez had made the same calculus. He decided not to share his insight with Jack, who was lying on his back nearby, apparently engrossed by the sight of the stars.

I lay on the ground, in the wood at the top of the hill. There seemed to me to be so many good things in the world, so much opportunity, and here I was, again, in the dark, in the middle of France, with danger all around. This time, it was true, I was not alone, but I was beginning to feel that I had had enough of conflict.

I was sure that Sausmarez was a good and honourable man and would not risk people without reason. His main purpose was to gain intelligence from us when we returned, without doubt, but he must have realised that if we were discovered, the French would assume that their plans were known and that their advantage of surprise was gone.

I was not like Snowden, who glories, or perhaps I should say relishes, the prospect of risk, of pitting his wits against an enemy, as he does at cards. When action is likely, Snowden becomes truly fearless. I do not. I did and do not believe that I am a coward, but I was beginning to abhor warfare. I had met many French people, and felt no more animosity to individuals from that nation than I did to some English persons. I knew that Boney had to be stopped from defeating England, and that it was my duty to help, but I hoped that when it became light, we could count the number of barges and men and clear out back to the coast as soon as we could.

There was a touch on my shoulder. In truth, not a touch, but the toe of a boot, gently applied. I looked up and saw Snowden silhouetted against a starry background.

"Getting light, Jack. Let's have a good look at the place."

I got up and joined Wain and Trezeguet. We crawled forwards a few yards through the wood, until we were on the edge of quite a steep cultivated slope. Ahead of us, the sky gradually lightened, and before us were the buildings we had seen under construction during out last, happier visit. We could see the canal, with its locks, and the lake, dark in the weak light. Drawn up on its shore was a long line of barges, of the same type as I had seen that morning from *Clementine*'s foretop in St Malo. I felt a surge of excitement, despite myself. So many barges. And the buildings, huge and impressive, and in the foreground lines of tents, enough to house probably thousands of troops.

Snowden nudged me. "We were right, Jack, or at least you were."

Wain beckoned, and we retreated on our hands and knees until we were well inside the wood. Looking round the bases of trees. Snowden started to count the barges under his breath. We could see now that the bank of the canal was crowded with them. Wain counted the tents. Snowden put up his spyglass, and was startled when Wain, moving quickly, knocked it away from his eye.

"Reflections," said Wain, and Snowden nodded.

"Sorry."

It was steadily becoming lighter, birds were singing in the trees, but there was no movement below us, and with the exception of one of the barrack chimneys, no smoke rising.

Wain looked at his watch, and then at us, and spoke quietly. "Reveille? My experience is that the French army is not in the habit of lying abed of a morning."

Snowden agreed. "Nor mine. Generally up with the lark."

We could see occasional figures moving in front of the buildings, but only a handful. Perhaps we had seen three or four, and they did not seem to move with great purpose. We watched for another half hour, but there was no more activity.

Trezeguet spoke, putting into words what we were all thinking. "The army is not there."

At that moment we were startled by sounds of a scuffle in the distance behind us, and Wain gestured to his sergeant to investigate. A few minutes later the man returned.

"Farmer, sir. Sentry spotted him."

We looked behind and saw a man, dressed like a peasant with wide canvas trousers, sitting on the ground as two of *Clementine*'s men stood beside him, a yoke with miraculously upright milk cans on the ground behind him. The sailors, who seemed to have effortlessly made the transition to soldiers, pointed bayoneted muskets at him. He seemed to be in an advanced state of shock, as well he might. The man started to speak, in what I recognised as Breton.

Wain spoke to the sailors. "Go easy, lads." The men lowered their muskets. "Can you talk to him, Trezeguet?"

"I will. Give us some space."

We moved back, and Trezeguet sat on the ground near the man and conversed rapidly in Breton for a few minutes.

"His name is Seznec," said Trezeguet, gesturing towards the captive, who seemed to have recovered himself somewhat. "He is a farmer. He lives alone, down there." He pointed in the presumed direction of Seznec's dwelling. "He was on his way to the barracks, he sells milk to them. Sometimes he walks through the woods as it is shorter for him."

"Ask him how many soldiers are there," said Wain.

There was another conversation in Breton, which Trezeguet interpreted for us. "He says that usually there are thousands of French soldiers there, he doesn't know how many, but a great number, but they have all gone."

"Does he know why they have gone, and where?"

A long monologue ensued from the prisoner, and when he had finished, Trezeguet translated again. I heard the word "Bonaparte" in the stream of Breton.

"He says he does not know where they have gone. He says that many people from here have been working for the French, building the canal and boats. The labourers came from the country and from Rennes, and the boat-builders from the coast, from Maloes. They say the canal will bring great trade. They have built many barges, and Bonaparte himself came to inspect them."

"Bonaparte?" interjected Wain.

The Chouan nodded, "Yes, Bonaparte."

"Bless my soul, very glad to have missed him."

I heartily endorsed this view, and Trezeguet continued.

"Bonaparte was very pleased with what he saw, there was a great dinner, and he gave a week's holiday to everybody. They have gone back to their homes, nearly all of them. A number of them even went by boat, along the canal."

Wain looked thoughtful. "Ask him about the soldiers."

There was another conversation in Breton.

"He says Bonaparte watched them land the barges on the lake, and it is said he even swam in the lake himself, and was covered in mud."

I thought of what Fulton had told me of Bonaparte. "That rings true, sir."

Wain nodded. "Please continue, Monsieur Trezeguet."

"He says that Bonaparte went off with all the soldiers. There are none here now. He does not know where they went, but they were headed towards the east. It is said that Bonaparte was very pleased with them."

Wain looked at us. "This is most extraordinary, gentlemen," and then back at Trezeguet: "Can he tell us who was in charge here?"

"A man called Bisset, a Frenchman, is in charge of the canal, and Morlaix, who is a Breton and should know better, is in command of the barges and the military. Morlaix went away with Bonaparte, but he does not know where Bisset is."

There was a loud exhalation of breath from Snowden. "Captain Wain, Stone, a word with you if I may, in private."

We walked a few paces with him, my heart sinking. I knew what he was thinking as he stopped and turned towards the marine. "Captain Wain, it seems to me that we have before us a great opportunity."

"How so, Snowden?"

I interjected, I hope in not too resigned a voice. "He believes, sir, that the French have left this place unguarded, and that we may be able to strike a blow, rather than just observe."

"Jack, my boy," said Snowden, "you're very perceptive this morning."

"What do you want to do?" asked Wain.

"Well, Captain Wain, before us we have the French invasion barges, enough to carry a great many men to certainly the Channel Islands and probably to England." He looked at me. "Stone and I know the man in charge of this operation, Captain Morlaix. Damn, man – Stone and I have been in his house in Paris. Jack will tell you that he's a formidable foe."

I nodded. I knew what he was going to propose, and in my heart realised that it was the right thing to do.

"It is clearly important there are so many barges and Bonaparte being here."

Snowden got to the heart of the matter. "Thank you, Jack. The fact is, Captain Wain, that for some reason the troops have been taken away …."

Wain held up his hand. "What are you suggesting, Snowden?" His voice was concerned, even suspicious.

"I say we stroll down there with a bit of kindling …."

"Stroll?" asked Wain, astonished, "with a bit of kindling?"

I could only echo Wain's surprise at Snowden's choice of vocabulary.

"Sorry, perhaps I spoke rather lightly. What I mean is that there are unguarded barges down there, and we have an opportunity to burn them. The weather has been fine for some time, they're new, the wood's dry and the pitch still pretty fresh. They'll go up like tinder. Obviously, as the commander of the military, you would decide how to approach. Mr Stone and I, as the naval representatives, will take care of the actual naval part of the operation, that is to set fire to as many barges as we can."

There it was; I knew we had to try.

Snowden had known, as soon as it got light and he looked down on the French establishment, that it was deserted, or almost so. What the French had achieved since Stone and he had passed that way was impressive. Permanent buildings, temporary sheds, and barges, perhaps a hundred of them, all alike, lined up on the shore of the lake or on the banks of the canal. But there were almost no people. There were lines and lines of tents, evenly spaced, but there was no smoke from cooking fires, no reveille call, no sergeants shouting to raise the men. And the building sheds, along the canal, surely these should have been busy with the start of the day's work by now. But they were quiet and, as far as he could see, smoke was only curling from one chimney in the whole place.

He felt excitement rising in him. It seemed too good to be true. Could the French really have left all those barges deserted? Careless wasn't the word for it; reckless more like.

And then they had interviewed the peasant. What a tale that was. Morlaix – they had known about that – but Boney as well? To leave this place deserted would surely have required some exceptional event, and probably a visit from Bonaparte would fit that. Why had he taken the soldiers, and were there any left?

Well, there it was, laid out at their feet. They had a good hand, but playing it effectively would mean a steady nerve, and a modicum of luck would be required. The question was, could he persuade Wain?

In his excitement, he had been too flippant – a *stroll, a bit of kindling*. He knew it was not going to be like that, and had mended his tone. He knew Jack realised that they had to follow such an opportunity, though he was beginning to think that Stone's spirit was not what it had once been.

He could see that Wain was thinking about what he had said.

"Upon my word, Snowden, this is extraordinary. We came here to verify the existence of this place, and to count the number of barges and troops …."

Snowden started to interrupt, but Wain held up his hand. "If I may finish, Snowden. As I said, we have verified that Froggie has an establishment here, and that there are a number of barges, apparently complete. Judging by the number of tents, there must be a substantial military presence here, usually that is. This intelligence, if we can get it back to Admiral Sausmarez, will be of the utmost importance. Those are our orders."

Snowden, resisting the temptation to shout at the marine, spoke rapidly. "If we get back and tell Sausmarez, the barges will still be here. Maloes will have to be blockaded, and that will tie up God knows how many of our ships and men. Wain, down there are more than a hundred of the things, packed together, lined up. The Lord alone knows how much all of this must have cost them, and they're here, unguarded. We can strike them the devil of a blow and still get back with our intelligence. A bold commander could …."

"Don't talk to me of your bold commanders, Snowden, I think I know all of that. I broke down the cabin door of the *San Nicholas* for Nelson at St Vincent."

Snowden, like all the Navy, and indeed all of the country, knew the story of Nelson's actions at the Battle of Cape St Vincent, where he had boarded two Spanish ships in succession, forcing their surrender.

"I didn't know that, Captain Wain. That must have been something to see. But we have an opportunity here, if we take it, immediately, now."

"I know we do, damn you, but we have our orders."

Snowden interrupted, "What would Nelson do here, Wain? What is it to be, orders or duty? If you don't do it, by God, I'll take the sailors and we'll …."

Jack interjected, "Stop, Percy, stop. That is most unfair. Wain has his orders and is in command; if you please, we'll have no more of that talk."

"I apologise, Wain, and I withdraw that remark, but …."

Wain's hand was at his forehead, and he sighed deeply. "No, Snowden, you are quite right. I know we have a chance, and I know very well what Nelson would do, damn you, I've seen him at close quarters, but I'm Wain, not Nelson."

"Very well."

Wain looked round and beckoned. "Sergeant Wilson, join us if you please."

Sergeant Wilson walked over to where we were standing.

"Sergeant, it seems that Froggie has left his invasion barges for us to do what we will. How are the men?"

"Tired, sir, but full of spirit I'd say."

"Well, Sergeant, I believe that that spirit will be tested to the full before the day is out."

"Sir?"

"We intend to fire those barges, Sergeant, and we'll have to be quick about it, before Boney's army comes back."

"Very well, sir. May I ask how we plan to do it?"

"You may indeed, Sergeant."

Chapter 22 – The Barges

Well, it was decided. I had really known all along that we could not ignore the chance, and that Snowden, the light in his eyes, would be more than a match for Wain. I really believed that if Wain had refused, Snowden was capable of taking the sailors and making an independent attempt on the barges.

While the sailors were gathering brushwood, Snowden took me aside. He gestured towards the French base below us, deserted in the sunshine.

"Jack, I know that perhaps I am putting you in peril. Capture could be bad for any of us, but for you …."

He was right. I thought of Fouché and shivered inwardly.

"Look, I've spoken to Wain, and we propose to send you back to the boats with Trezeguet and a couple of men. When you get to the boats you can take one and carry the news."

The thought of the trip through France, pretty well by myself, filled me with horror.

"No, Perce, it won't do, and you know it. It would take more than a couple of men to get those boats into the water, at least quickly. And before you go and say anything, I'd be obliged if you didn't suggest that we could steal a boat. I've had enough of that. No, I'll stay with you, for better or worse."

"Very well, Jack."

In the midday sun, we walked quietly between hedgerows towards the lake. Snowden, investigating before our departure, had reported that the lane beside the hill leading towards the lake was sufficiently sunken to make men in it invisible from the boatyard. From time to time we stopped to allow the men scouting ahead to drop back and report, the sailors pleased to lay down their bundles of brushwood for a moment. The men seemed completely unconcerned about their situation, as men frequently do when they have faith in their commanders, and bolstered as we were in those days by the sometimes unthinking and unfounded confidence in the Navy's invincibility.

And then, suddenly, we were at the lake, the line of barges drawn up on the shore near us. They seemed huge, as ships ashore do when viewed from the ground near them, and some had ladders leaning against their hulls. The scale of the enterprise was impressive, I thought, as I knelt under my burden while Wain and Snowden looked through the hedges.

Wain nodded, and suddenly we were running across open ground towards the barges. When we reached them, the marines continued, spreading out, and lay on the ground facing away from the barges, sighting along their muskets.

I climbed up the ladder of the nearest barge, immediately struck by the smell of new tar and timber. The barge was rather roughly made, but its obvious purposefulness made it somehow impressive. I thought to myself of the wastefulness of it all, as I crouched under a thwart, striking a light with my tinder box onto some of the brushwood I had brought.

The fire was well alight and the thwart was beginning to burn fiercely when I threw myself down the ladder. Several of the barges were starting to burn, and I decided to move well along the line, so as to start a blaze in a new section of the line of barges.

I was crouched down in the bottom of the barge, blowing on what was becoming quite a promising fire, when I heard yelling from the direction of the buildings, and then a distant musket shot. We were discovered. I left the fire and swung down over the side of the barge to the ground. The French musketry had started to become more frequent, and I heard a ball strike the hull of the barge behind me, but our men had not yet replied.

I saw Snowden, cutlass in hand, and I thought, in his element, gambling, the smoke from the burning barges roiling about him.

He shouted above the crackle of the flames behind him, "One more apiece, come on lads," waving his cutlass in the direction of the unburnt barges.

I ran, thinking that at least my load of brushwood was getting less, and climbed into a barge, a long way down the line, closer to the buildings. By now the musketry was becoming intense, and our men were firing back. I knelt down in the bilges of the barge, concentrating on starting the fire, when I heard Wain's voice.

"Fall back, come on men."

I was not reluctant to retire, and I waited until the fire was well established, and stood up to climb out of the barge. As I stood, I felt a tremendous blow on my shoulder, and then an intense numbing pain. My sight dimmed, and I felt the wood of the barge's deck hit my forehead, feeling strangely soft. After some time, I don't know how long, perhaps minutes, I awoke and lay there. The barge was burning fiercely about me, I was choking in the smoke, and the heat of the fire was intense.

I heard Wain's voice from below, amongst the musket shots. "Stone, are you in there? By God man, get out."

I could make no reply, but heard the sound of someone climbing the rail, Wain.

"There you are, Stone, let's get you out of here, damned hot."

I felt strong arms under my shoulders, and I was half carried, half dragged down the side of the barge, my shoulder screaming with pain. As though in a dream I took in the burning barges, the flames, the thick smoke, musket shots. Wain laid me on the ground, and then, with a grunt, knelt and draped me over his shoulder, like a sack of grain. He stood and started to run, but before he had gone a few paces, shrieked and fell. I knew no more.

We were in the lane. Sergeant Wilson, with some of his men, had formed a rearguard, their muskets levelled over the edge of the bank of the lane. It was plain that the attention of the French was entirely on the barges, attempting to get those that were not on fire off the shore and into the lake. But the men were few and the barges heavy.

Wilson stood up and Snowden beckoned him over. "Sergeant Wilson, over here please."

"Midshipman Stone and Captain Wain are not here, and one of the ABs is missing. How have your marines fared?"

"Sir, one of the men saw Wain attempting to carry Stone, but Wain was hit, and they are still back there. We've lost two of the men, probably wounded."

"Are there any serious injuries here?"

"No, sir, nothing that will stop men marching. And sir, begging your pardon, it may become very unhealthy hereabouts soon, and perhaps we should be thinking about putting some distance between us and this place."

"Yes, Wilson, you are quite right. Damn, I wish we hadn't lost Stone, or Wain. I'm afraid it was my fault, we …." Snowden hung his head. He felt crushed, devastated. The memory of Jack's parents at their cottage in Portland came into his head, and he remembered what Jack had said: *'Twas a famous victory*.

"Begging your pardon again, sir, with respect, we don't have time for that. What's done is done, and we've made a pretty good bonfire." He leaned closer to Snowden and whispered, fiercely. "Sir, just get your arse to the head of the column, and lead – that's your duty now. We must get on the road."

Snowden nodded and said quietly, "Of course, sergeant." He moved away and turned back to Wilson, his voice strong.

"Sergeant, are we ready?"

"Aye aye, sir," and then in a loud voice, "come on you men, let's get moving. Double. You know the drill, hundred and hundred."

The bedraggled column moved along the lane, to the north, towards the sea and away from the flames and smoke.

She had been in her bedroom, packing for her return to Paris, when several things happened very quickly. From the direction of the yard she heard shouting, followed by the sound of musketry, and Madame Peress rushed into the room, red with excitement.

"The English are here, they are attacking the French. Come quickly, let us go to the cellar and hide."

The English? How could that be? Not now, no, when Bonaparte had taken away the soldiers! Dominique's pulse raced, but her mind was steady.

"The cellar cannot be locked. Do you not remember that the door was damaged last week by the carter when he was delivering cider?"

"We can hide amongst the barrels, Dominique."

"I think that is a very bad idea. No harm will come to us if we wait here."

As Dominique spoke, they heard a window downstairs shatter. Peress flinched, as she might well, for Dominique knew that the time of rebellion had been hard on her and her family.

"Keep away from the window, Dominique, we should lie on the floor. The walls are thick and will protect us." The sounds of battle intensified as they lay there, until Dominique could resist temptation no longer.

"Dominique, get down," said Peress, in an unnecessary whisper, as she crawled over to the window and peered around its corner towards the lake, from where she could see a great column of smoke billowing up. The barges, her father's work, were on fire.

She could not help herself. "Damn him," she shouted, "damn him."

"Come away from the window and lie down."

Dominque lay on the floor again.

"Damn who, Dominique?"

"That cursed Bonaparte, Peress. My father warned him that the barges were open to attack if he took the troops away, and they have been attacked. My father says he is reckless, and lost many of our men in Egypt for no reason, and now he has undone all of my father's work."

Peress, who Dominique suspected was not unequivocally loyal to the Republic, muttered something unintelligible.

The firing died down, then stopped, and after a while Dominique risked another trip to the window, just in time to glimpse the end of a ragged body of men trot past in the lane and disappear northwards. The English. There did not seem to be very many of them. Towards the lake, the smoke was thick, rising in waves.

"They have gone, Peress, I have just seen the English go past in the lane, but the barges are burning."

"Stay where you are, Dominique, there may be more of them."

She did not think so, and went down to the hall.

"Where are you going, Dominique?"

"To the barracks of course, to see how things are."

"Wait an hour or so, there may still be fighting."

"I will take my chance. I am sure the English have gone, and there is no fighting."

She ran across to the barracks. The line of barges at the lake was burning fiercely, and the air was full of acrid smoke and falling ashes. She went across the bridge near the lock gates and into the barracks. There was only one person in the lobby, a sailor who she recognised, standing by the door to the refectory, through which she could hear horrible groans.

"Who is in there?" she asked the sailor.

"The wounded, Mademoiselle Morlaix, ours and the English." He stood aside, and she opened the door to be met with a ghastly sight. There were perhaps twenty wounded men in the room, lying or sitting on the floor, some with terrible wounds visible.

She looked round at the sailor. "What is being done for them?"

He shrugged. "Everybody is at the lake, the fire, Mademoiselle."

"The surgeon, where is he?"

"I believe he and his assistants went off with the army, Mademoiselle. My orders are to guard the door. There are English in there as well as our men."

She thought to herself of the horror of the situation, with men in urgent need of attention and the surgeon taken away by the imbecile Bonaparte (from then on, she always mentally prefaced the word Bonaparte with "imbecile"). She remembered the surgeon, Quiniou, who lived quietly in a small house near her own, and who dealt in an unaffected way with the illnesses of the local population. Would he help? He had a reputation for turning out at any time of the night to help anyone in need, and for refusing payment from the poor.

She ran, through the smoke, across the bridge and up the hill, past her house, and hammered on the door of Quiniou's residence. She saw an upstairs curtain move, and moments later an elderly woman, who she presumed was his wife, cautiously opened the door.

"Is Monsieur Quiniou here?" she almost shouted.

The woman shrunk back slightly, nodded and disappeared into the house. Dominique noticed that she limped as she moved. A moment later, Quiniou, a short, elderly, balding man, stood at the door.

"Mademoiselle Morlaix, I think."

"Yes, sir."

"How can I help?"

"The English have attacked. At the barracks there are many wounded men. There is no surgeon, and …." Her voice trailed off.

The old man suddenly seemed to increase in stature. "Of course, please wait while I gather my things."   He turned to go.

"Monsieur, the men have no bedding. Shall I go to my house and gather up some things? It is on your way, can you meet me there?"

"Very well."

She ran back, shouting as she hammered on the door for Peress to open it.

"Peress, come here."

"Coming, Dominique."

"We must get all the linen and blankets from the house and put them into the handcart."

"Why, Dominique?"

"There are wounded men in the barracks, and they seem to have no bedding – they are just lying on the floor of the refectory. Quiniou is going to take charge, he will be here in a minute."

"A good doctor. The poor men, I thought we had done with war, but that *sale* Corsican has brought it here."

She reached down to the keys on her belt and opened the door of the linen store. In a few minutes, the store's contents had been transferred to the handcart which was kept in the cellar.

They were loading bottles of brandy from the cellar into the cart when Quiniou arrived, carrying a pair of large bags. He looked at them as he added his bags to the load on the cart.

"You have done well – will you help me with the cart to the barracks, Mademoiselle Morlaix? I fear it would be difficult for me to get it over the bridge by myself."

"Of course, Monsieur Quiniou."

"Shall I help, doctor?" asked Peress.

"No, if you would be so kind as to go to my house and assist my wife. She is packing some more supplies, and it would be useful if you could help her, she has rheumatism very badly."

Peress nodded and set off towards the surgeon's house.

Dominique and Quiniou each took one side of the handcart's handle. Before long it was clear that Quiniou was struggling with the load, and they stopped.

"Monsieur Quiniou," asked Dominique "are you well?" She was shocked by the grey colour of his face. The surgeon rested against the side of the cart.

"Sadly, I am not. An old wound makes my back exceedingly painful if I exert myself. I fear pushing this cart has not been beneficial to it."

"Do not worry, Monsieur Quiniou, I am sure that I can manage the cart. It is downhill apart from the bridge."

They set off again. Dominique pushed the cart, with Quiniou walking, stooped beside it.

"You have known war, Monsieur Quiniou?" she asked when they reached a smooth part of the track.

"Sadly, yes. I was a military surgeon for several years, until I received my wound and was invalided. I was glad in a way, I have had enough of violence." He looked at Dominique as she strained at the handle of the cart. "Will you help me when we get there? My wife will arrive shortly, but she can hardly walk with the rheumatism, and her asthma makes her very short of breath. A fine couple we are!"

"Of course, Monsieur Quiniou, I will do what I can."

"That is good, you will carry some authority because of your father's position. That will certainly help."

As she struggled with the cart, the surgeon explained what would have to be done to help the wounded. "First, we must make beds..."

Chapter 25 – North? No, South

Snowden, at the head of the ragged column, began to recover. He knew that the rebuke from Sergeant Wilson had been well deserved, and even essential, and his mind turned to practical problems. The Chouan, Trezeguet, walked beside him, exhausted, the paleness of his face emphasised by the black smudges of soot across it, but his blue eyes alight with fanaticism.

"You have done very well, Snowden. You have struck such a blow against the French and their plans."

"At a cost though, Trezeguet."

"That is true, but we have burnt no cottages or crops, and killed no peasants. That is the nature of the republicans who we fight."

"Trezeguet, as I remember, the road passes through several villages on our way back to the boats, and it will be daylight for much of the time. Will it be possible for us to go round them? The men are exhausted."

"No, Snowden, it will not be possible for us to bypass them, it will take too long, and as you say, the men are exhausted. We do not have time. The French army has gone, I do not know where, or how far, but the Corsican was with them, and I have no doubt that he will be full of revenge. Speed is our ally."

"But the villages."

"We will march boldly through, in good order. The people will look away."

Snowden called Sergeant Wilson up from the rear of the column. They stopped by a stream, and the men rested briefly and cleaned themselves up as best they could.

As Trezeguet had predicted, at the first village the few people who were about either went indoors when they saw the English approach or looked on impassively from the side of the road. They were nearly clear of the second village when a man dressed in the clothes of a peasant came up and pulled Trezeguet to the side. An out-of-breath Trezeguet caught up shortly and spoke urgently.

"Snowden, bad news I am afraid. That man, an old fighter, has told me that our boats have been discovered, and that he believes soldiers will be there shortly. We cannot use them."

Snowden thought hard, and after a few minutes signalled a halt. The men followed him through a hedge into a small field, off the road. He called Wilson over and they sat with Trezeguet.

"Wilson, the boats have been found, I am afraid. We cannot use them."

Wilson gave no outward sign of concern. "I am sorry to hear that, sir. Do you have an alternative plan?"

"It seems to me that there are two alternatives." Trezeguet leaned forwards as Snowden spoke. "We can continue northwards, and walk seawards as far as we can, and hope to make ourselves visible to the ship. However, that seems to me to be difficult, as there may be soldiers waiting, and the ship will be standing well off from the land."

Trezeguet interjected, "Impossible, Snowden, the beach is guarded there, and the soldiers will have seen what went on at St Malo. They will be alert."

Snowden knew that it was true that the French would guard the beach there, as it had been the site of British incursions before, and indeed a disastrous attempt to evacuate a British force in 1780.

"It seems to me that a better chance is for us to head to the west, to Quiberon. There is often a British squadron in the bay, and I believe there is a network ashore which is friendly towards us."

Trezeguet held up his hands in a violent gesture. "No, again, impossible. The republicans are everywhere there. There have been so many interventions. We will get nowhere near the coast."

Wilson agreed. "He is right there, sir. I was at Quiberon in '97. The place was crawling with the French then. We were lucky to get away."

"Many of my people did not get away," said Trezeguet.

"Where, then?" asked Snowden, feeling a tide of despair rising in him.

"I am not sure, but perhaps further south. The Vilaine. There are fewer soldiers there, and we may be able to get passage on a boat out to sea."

Snowden thought, trying to picture the geography in his head. He remembered the action at Quiberon, but his ship had taken little part in it, and he was very young at the time. He remembered the Vilaine estuary, or the mouth of it, just about. Shallow and rather hostile, he thought, but as far as he could remember, pretty lonely, the coast indistinct, low lying. He had no knowledge of the Vilaine itself, but presumed it was tidal and muddy.

"The people there, Trezeguet, what are their sympathies?"

"It is hard to generalise, Snowden, but there are many who have no love for the Republic."

"The roads?"

"They are not too bad, and mostly quite lonely. We will have to bypass Rennes."

Snowden shivered. The sun was setting, and the wind blowing colder. "Very well, then. To the Vilaine it is." Snowden went over to where the men were sitting, and told them of the situation. They seemed rather apathetic about it. When he had finished, to an accompaniment of groans, Wilson got the men on their feet, and, under Trezeguet's direction, they moved across a series of fields and woods to another road, which headed roughly west, towards the setting sun. They set out, slowly now, the men all in.

Snowden spotted a barn near what was, for the district, quite a large house.

"The barn there, Trezeguet, I think it would be good to get the men inside for a few hours. What do you think?"

Snowden led the men to the barn. It was a mean building, with a low, patched roof, but it was out of the wind, and the men immediately threw off their accoutrements and lay down in the straw, exhausted. Only Sergeant Wilson was alert, posting himself just outside the door.

He spoke to Snowden. "Do you think, sir, we could forage up some vittles? The men have just about finished their biscuit. That farm down there looks quite prosperous, must have a store laid in."

Snowden turned to Trezeguet. "What do you think?"

"I will try." He held out his hand. "Some coin, if you please."

Snowden handed over some gold, and Trezeguet got ready to leave.

Wilson watched him. "With your permission, sir, I suggest Corporal Corbin accompanies Monsieur Trezeguet, just to make sure he comes to no harm."

Snowden looked hard at him. "Very well, Wilson, but I think if Trezeguet …." He suddenly realised what Wilson meant. "Yes, of course, have Corporal Corbin accompany Monsieur Trezeguet."

Trezeguet, accompanied by Corbin, set off towards the farm.

Snowden spoke to Wilson. "Look here, Wilson, I appreciate your concerns, but if Trezeguet was going to betray us, he'd have done it by now, surely?"

"Perhaps, sir, but I was at Quiberon, and I saw them all fighting between themselves, every man out for himself it seemed like. And we only have his word for the boats being discovered."

The thought hit Snowden like a blow as Wilson continued. "I'd like to roust the men out, ready like, just in case."

"Yes, Wilson, no doubt you're right to be concerned. Stand the men to."

Time dragged on, tension rising in Snowden's breast, until they heard the sound of footsteps coming up the hill towards the barn, clearly making no attempt at concealment. Trezeguet entered, followed by Corbin and a boy of about twelve. They carried sacks with food and a cask of what was evidently cider. Trezeguet looked round at the men with their weapons at the ready, peeking through gaps in the wall of the barn. He nodded in understanding and turned to Snowden.

"You may have no fear of me, Lieutenant. I will not tell you now of what the revolutionaries did to my family, but suffice it to say that I would rather burn in hell than help them."

"Well said, Trezeguet, but I have to be careful."

"I know that Wilson distrusts me."

"Perhaps he does."

A thought, unworthy, crossed Snowden's mind. "The boy, shall we keep him?"

"No, Lieutenant, you shall not. I will not be party to taking my fellow Bretons hostage."

Chapter 26 – The Encounter

The next few hours were the most exhausting of her life, and in her memory thereafter seemed like a descent into hell. A sickening smell of smoke pervaded everything, and the air was full of ash as the barges continued to burn. The wounded men groaned and whimpered in pain.

With the help of a couple of sailors, Dominique improvised beds, and helped lift the men onto them. Peress arrived, and they gave the men water, or brandy and water if they seemed restless. They carried a large table from the refectory into a side room, and Monsieur Quiniou arranged his instruments on a sideboard. The surgeon had told Dominique what he intended to do, and she accompanied him as he went round the room, examining the men, usually with a quiet word of encouragement. He called it triage, which meant that he decided who would benefit from treatment first; she thought it was deciding who should be left to die.

The horror of the first hours was indescribable as she assisted Quiniou with the men on the table. Some, no all, of the injuries were horrible; the men, who a few hours before had been strong and confident, seemed weak and frightened, like sick children. Quiniou, despite his age and infirmities, moved with such speed and skill that it was impossible for Dominique to understand what he was doing. She fumbled at his instructions, cutting away clothing, pressing pads of cloth to bleeding wounds, cleaning and tying. Her hands were red with blood, but they did not shake. Peress was strong, comforting the men, giving them water and the precious laudanum, and under the direction of Madame Quiniou, sitting on a chair, applying bandages and compresses.

Peress came into the side room. Dominique did not know how long she had been in that room, but when she looked at the window, she saw it was dusk outside.

"Only one left, Monsieur Quiniou. Shall we bring him in now?"

"If you please."

She and a sailor brought the man into the room. Dominique could see that he was hardly more than a boy, his face blackened and his hair almost singed off. He seemed familiar to her, and she assumed he was probably a sailor from the barges. They laid him on the table, and she put a pillow under his head. As Quiniou examined him, poking at his body, and talking to himself, she sponged off his face. He moaned slightly, but seemed deeply unconscious, with a horrible wound in his right shoulder, and his left leg at a strange angle. As she sponged off his face, she realised that the eyelashes had melted together, keeping them shut. She washed him as well as she could, and stood back to await the surgeon's instructions, looking at the injured man's face. It was not what is commonly described as a shock of recognition, but rather as though her mind was assembling pieces of a puzzle, which slowly formed a picture. There could be no doubt ….

Quiniou spoke, "I didn't think this one would last an hour, but he must be tougher than he looks. Peress has done well with that shoulder. I think …."

Dominique turned to him. "Monsieur Quiniou – is that an English uniform?"

"Well, yes, I believe it is, but …."

"I know him."

"What?"

"He is Jack Stone. I met him at my mother's house in Paris."

He looked at her. "Are you sure? You must be strong my dear." He shook his head. "He is in a bad way I fear. But, well, he has survived so far, which I did not expect. Would you like me to ask Peress to replace you?"

"No, I will help."

"Let us cut away his shirt – there is no exit wound, so the ball, I believe he has caught a musket ball, must be inside him."

They went to work. From time to time she whispered in Jack's ear. She was sure that he could not hear her, but even if he could not, doing so helped her.

"Don't worry, Jack, soon you will be better."

"Monsieur Quiniou is a good man."

"We are nearly finished now."

Between them, using the surgeon's instruments and their fingers, they got hold of the flattened musket ball and managed to remove it from Jack's shoulder. The next stage was equally horrible, looking in the wound for pieces of cloth from his clothes, which the surgeon said was just as important. When they had finished, they worked to set his leg.

Eventually it was done, and Quiniou straightened up. "Well, Dominique, your man has survived the operation, and the ball is removed. We must chance to providence now."

She remembered that night as though it was a dream. The men, groaning, but quieter now, the fire outside gradually dying down, Quiniou on a sofa with his wife beside him, both exhausted, sleeping. Dominique was exhausted too, but she could not sleep. She could hardly take her eyes off Jack, staring, fascinated at the rise and fall of his chest, willing his breathing to continue.

They were sitting outside a pleasant house near Dol when a rider galloped up, dismounted without tethering his horse, and rushed up to the table. Murat and Napoléon's aides stood and reached for their swords, but Napoléon and Morlaix remained seated, calm and serene.

"The English, First Consul, the English are attacking St Malo."

Morlaix had ridden through the night, with Napoléon and Murat, at the head of a detachment of Guards. As they neared St Malo, the glow in the sky became more evident, and the sound of bombardment increased.

"Sounds like thirty-two pounders," said Morlaix, "a ship of the line." He looked at the red trace of rockets overhead, "And a bomb ship as well."

"Serious, then," said Napoléon. "They tried before, I think in '88."

Murat spurred his horse.

"Steady," said Bonaparte, "a few minutes will make no difference."

By midnight they were standing on the ramparts of the fort with the town's commander, Dassault.

"The English are putting on a fine show, Dassault," Bonaparte remarked, as the warship just offshore fired a broadside, the orange flames momentarily lighting her against the dark background.

"First Consul," replied Dassault, "do you believe they plan to invade?"

"If they do, my Guards will give them a welcome they won't forget, eh Murat?"

"They certainly will," the general replied.

In the flash of the guns, Morlaix thought he had seen a ship, a small vessel, quite close in under the ramparts. He watched intently, and when a fire flared up ashore he saw her again, not distinctly, but there was no doubt in his mind.

"There's an English ship, just there. I don't know what she's about, but it could be a fireship. It is what I would do if I was attacking this place. I'll take some of the *marins* and see what can be done." The *marins* were sailors who had been recruited into the Guards, soldiers as well as sailors.

He ran back along the ramparts, turning as he heard footsteps behind him – Murat.

"I am with you, Morlaix."

"Have you ever been in a boat …?" As he spoke, he realised that the question he was about to ask would just waste time, and he was sure that time was short. Murat may not have had much nautical experience, but Morlaix knew that he was a good man to have beside you in a fight. "Very well."

They ran on. At the quay there was a good-sized boat, perhaps twenty feet long.

"This one will do. Get a few *marins*."

Murat sprinted off, towards the Guards who were engaged in fighting fires, passing buckets along a line of men from the harbour. Morlaix got in the boat and started shipping the rowlocks and casting off the mooring lines. When Murat arrived with the men, the boat was ready. Morlaix could see no sign of the ship, but he was sure that it would be heading towards the moored frigates.

They were good seamen, the *marins*, and the boat was soon underway, with Morlaix steering. Murat was in the bows, one hand shading his eyes, when he shouted, "There!" and pointed. A small flame was visible in the darkness. It grew in intensity, and before long Morlaix could see it outlining the sails and rigging of a ship. The ship was not moving quickly, but even with Morlaix urging the rowers on, the boat overhauled her only slowly.

By the time they were twenty yards from the English ship, the blaze aboard had grown dramatically. They were not far from the moored French frigates, which were alive with activity, futile activity he thought. There was nothing they could do to escape in the time available, and it would be difficult to prevent the spread of fire if the burning ship collided with them.

Outlined by the flames, Morlaix could see a solitary man at the fireship's wheel, staring ahead, occasionally giving the helm a spoke, and sometimes glancing up at the fire which was beginning to lick round the lower rigging. Morlaix clenched his fists. "Come on lads, twenty yards, then we'll have them."

The boat surged ahead, and the bow bumped against the side of the ship.

"The painter," shouted Morlaix, too late, as Murat leaped, grabbed the side of the ship, and heaved himself up over the rail. The boat, in reaction to Murat's leap, separated from the ship. A couple of rowers on the port side, who had left their seats and were crouching, ready to board the ship, sat back down and brought the boat back alongside.

Morlaix scrambled onto the ship with the men, arriving just in time to see the man who had been at the wheel dive over the rail into the sea. The state of the ship was shocking, a scene from hell. The heat from the fire was intense, and the noise tremendous, a horrible roaring and crackling. He ran to the wheel, cut through the lashing, and put the helm down. The ship came up into the wind, blowing the flames and heat back on the men around the wheel. They recoiled, the ship was slowing. He knew what had to be done. He started to shout "Lee braces" to bring the foresail round, but as he did it burst into flames.

He checked himself. The ship was fore and aft rigged on the mainmast. "Bring the mainsheet in," he yelled, and men moved aft and started to haul the mainsail in. The ship steadied on her course, and started to make headway, towards the opposite side of the Rance, where there was nothing that could be damaged.

"Into the boat, quick, don't cast off," he shouted, and the men, not needing much urging, climbed over the rail and into the boat. Murat stood by his side at the wheel. The heat was almost intolerable now, and Morlaix busied himself with lashing the helm, making sure the ship was on course.

"Over you go, General," said Morlaix.

"After you, Breton," Murat replied.

They could not see the shore because of the glare of the fire, but Morlaix thought it must be close, and his supposition was confirmed when there was a crashing noise, and the ship heeled over.

"Aground," he said to Murat. "She's not going anywhere now."

As they turned to run to the boat there was a huge explosion. Morlaix felt a terrible blow on his left leg and a lesser blow as his head hit the deck; he had sufficient time before unconsciousness came to feel dreadful pain, and then hands under his shoulders, dragging him across the deck.

That night, Dominique had moved around the improvised hospital room as if in a dream. The men occasionally groaned or cried out, but they were certainly quieter than they had been before Quiniou had attended to them and had dosed some with laudanum. The surgeon had told her that Jack, her Jack as she thought of him now, was the only one about whom he was really concerned, and she hardly took her eyes off him.

By the morning he was feverish, restless, and the laudanum, what little they could get down him, seemed to have little effect.

"The next few hours, Dominique, will be critical," said Quiniou. "We must keep his body warm in the blankets, but his face cool."

She was sponging Jack's face when she looked up and saw Bisset standing by the bed. "Good morning, Miss Morlaix," he said.

"I am afraid it is not a very good morning at all," she replied.

"I am sorry, of course it is not. It is terrible. Will you step out for a minute, Dominique?"

They went outside, into the bright morning. The air was acrid with the smell of burning wood.

"Dominique, I have to return to Paris, to report to the board of the canal company. Fortunately, there is no damage to the canal, but even so they will expect a report in person."

"Very well, I shall see you on your return."

"Dominique, did your father not instruct you to go to Paris? I think that I should accompany you there."

"I have work to do here – the wounded."

"Dominique," he spoke to the girl as though she was incapable of understanding, "your father, Captain Morlaix, instructed you to go to Paris. You should obey him. It is your duty to go, and mine to take you."

He put out his hand as though to take hold of her arm. She pulled back quickly, out of his way, and she saw his eyes narrow. She was very tired, almost lightheaded, and she spoke without thinking, more harshly than she intended.

"You speak of duty. Duty! Where have you been? You seem to have been absent when there was hazardous work to do.

And now you are scuttling back to Paris. Well, go if you wish, I am needed here, looking after Jack and the others."

He looked affronted, as well he might. He had just gone off for a holiday like almost everybody else, he had not intentionally neglected his duty, and indeed he was a civilian.

"Jack? Who is Jack?"

"Twice the man you are."

He turned on his heel and walked away, his face flushed.

The next morning was just as grim. Jack's wound was inflamed and hot to the touch. His fever intensified, his face ran with sweat, and he was restless, delirious, talking nonsense. Quiniou was sure that there was nothing more that could be done.

"We took everything from the wound that we could find, Dominique, and if there is something still inside, well, we cannot get it now."

Dominique looked at him enquiringly, the question unspoken.

"He is young, strong. That counts in his favour. He has a good chance."

On the evening of the second day, Jack was especially disturbed, but eventually fell into a deep sleep. His breathing gradually became more regular as she sat with him.

Quiniou looked at his patient. "I believe the crisis has passed, Dominique. There is a long road to travel, but he has reached the end of the first part of the journey."

As dawn broke, Jack's eyes opened and he looked up at Dominique. He smiled faintly and whispered in what he probably thought was French: "Dominique. I knew you were here."

She could not stop herself from leaning forward and kissing his forehead. He smiled and went back to sleep.

By the middle of the day, he was propped up on pillows and taking small amounts of food. She knew that he and his fellow wounded Englishmen had burnt her father's barges, but she felt no anger towards them. She knew that her father would have done the same if the tables had been turned.

Blessed with youth's optimism, she remembered the rest of that day as one of the happiest times of her life. Jack's strength seemed to increase with every passing hour, and by the time she left him, at about ten in the evening, a strong bond had formed between them. She visited twice during the night, and each time he was sleeping soundly, his face pale but composed.

At about six in the morning, Dominique was awakened by a loud knock on the door, followed by a discussion between the caller and Peress. She went down the stairway and saw a naval officer standing in the hall. Her heart sank into despair.

"Mademoiselle Morlaix?"

"Yes, how can I help you?"

"It is your father, Captain Morlaix."

"Oh, no!" she whispered.

"Do not alarm yourself unduly, mademoiselle. The Captain is injured, gravely, but he is alive, and as the saying goes, there is hope."

"Injured, how?"

"The English attacked at St Malo, as I see they have done here." He gestured towards the lake. "Your father, with General Murat, boarded an English fireship with great gallantry. I believe a cannon exploded and wounded your father. General Murat ordered me here, to ask you to accompany me to him in St Malo. I have a fast boat ready on the canal."

"Your boat is at the wharf?"

"It is, Mademoiselle Morlaix."

"Then I will meet you there in an hour."

"Very well, mademoiselle." He turned and left the house, no doubt in search of breakfast.

Half an hour later she went into the barracks and sat by Jack's bed. She watched his calm face as he slept, perhaps as a mother does her child, feeling a great surge of love. She touched his hand and he woke, his eyes looking up at her.

"Good morning, Dominique."

"How are you this morning, Jack? You seemed to be sleeping very soundly."

"Such a sleep, Dominique! I am feeling much better, thank you."

"Jack, I have come to say goodbye to you."

His face fell. "Goodbye?"

"Yes, I am sorry, but Monsieur Quiniou says that you will recover. It will not be quick, but it is certain."

He nodded, and she reached out and took his hand. "Jack, my father has been wounded. At St Malo. There was an attack, and he was on a fireship. I do not know any more, but I must go to him. There is a boat outside, waiting to take me along the canal."

He grimaced, and she saw tears start in his eyes. "I know – they were planning an attack, as a diversion …." He stopped, perhaps thinking that he had said too much.

She could not help herself. "Damn this war. I hate it. What is the point of it?"

"Dominique, there is no point to war."

For the first time she heard him quote, but did not understand: "*But 'twas a famous victory.*"

"What?"

"A poem, *After Blenheim*. I don't know if it has been translated."

"Jack, I must go to my father now. I will see you again, I promise."

"I very much hope so, Dominique. Thank you for all you have done."

She leaned forwards and whispered in his ear, "I love you." She kissed him lightly on the lips and held his hand. "Goodbye Jack."

He gestured for her to lean forward again and whispered, "I love you too, Dominique, goodbye."

She walked over to the boat lying at the wharf, bag in hand, overcome by sadness, but at the same time something like elation.

Sergeant Wilson set pickets and distributed the food that had been brought to the men, some of whom fell asleep while eating. Snowden sat with Trezeguet, planning tomorrow's journey, but before long they too were fast asleep. Though he was dead tired, Wilson forced himself to sleep lightly, from time to time going outside to satisfy himself that all was well.

He roused them at dawn, and before long they were on what passed for a road, marching, if not briskly, then at a respectable pace. Snowden and Trezeguet were in the lead, with Snowden making frequent recourse to his compass. From time to time they came to a village, but they formed up and marched through each one in what Snowden thought was a fairly respectable way, and the few people about went inside or ignored them in a studied way. Snowden asked Trezeguet if the people were likely to betray them, but he shrugged.

"There are some who would, and others who would punish them for so doing. I do not know what will happen. We must hope for the best."

By midday, the sun was hot, and Snowden could see that the men were beginning to flag. He spied a stream ahead and signalled for Wilson to join him in the van of the party.

"Should we stop here, Wilson?"

"Aye, sir, I think we should. The men are just about beat." He nodded. "I'm thinking, perhaps a couple of hours, get past the hottest part of the day. We've made good progress so far."

"We have, seventeen miles by my reckoning, Wilson."

"I'll get the men well off the road."

"Very well."

The men were sitting by the side of the stream, in the shade of a wood, when they heard the shout of a sentry, followed by a noisy chase which ended when a very young man, followed by a breathless sentry, ran into the middle of the group of men.

"Sorry Sergeant," said the sentry, "I tried to stop him, but he's devilish fast."

As he was speaking, the young man, who had clearly identified Snowden as an officer, addressed him in rapid Breton. Snowden held up his hands to stop the flow of words, and they were shortly joined by Trezeguet, who interpreted.

"He has been sent by his father, an old Chouan, to warn us that there are French soldiers on the road, marching north."

Trezeguet spoke to the boy again. "He says that they are perhaps two leagues distant."

"Ask him how he knew we are here."

"He says that everybody knows. You march through the villages, you hide in the woods, disturb the birds."

Snowden looked at Wilson and grimaced.

"He says you must move away from the road. If you do, the French will not see you."

Snowden said to Wilson, "That seems to be good advice."

"It does, sir."

Wilson moved the men well away from the road, and they concealed themselves as best they could. After what seemed like a very long time, they heard the sound of an approaching column – marching men, horses and the rumble of gun carriages or baggage carts. They did not see the column, but to Snowden its passing seemed to take an age, during which he hardly dared to breathe. By his judgement, he waited half an hour after the last cart had passed, and then walked quietly by himself to the road, signalling to the men he passed to keep their heads down. He looked carefully in both directions, and listened intently, but apart from a cloud of dust in the distance, the column was not visible.

Snowden went back. "Seems clear, Sergeant."

"Very good, sir."

"Unpleasant experience."

"Very nasty indeed, sir. Let's hope we don't meet any more of them."

"Best to press on I think, Sergeant, it only needs one informer to tell them that they've seen us, and they'll turn round and be after us."

"True enough, sir, but a column on the march has definite orders to get somewhere, and they'd probably take a bit of convincing that the locals had really seen a party of English marching along the road."

"Let's hope you're right, Sergeant. Get the men on the road – double time if you please."

It started to rain, but they made good time for the rest of the day. There was no sign of any pursuit, and the people that they saw seemed indifferent to their passing. Snowden's idea had been to spend the night in the open, but because of the rain he decided that they should get under cover for the night, and before long found a promising-looking barn. Wilson went with Trezeguet to find and negotiate with the owner, and they were able to scavenge up enough food to make a reasonable meal, with the men, as before, immediately falling asleep.

Snowden sat with Wilson as Trezeguet explained their position. "I think that tomorrow, if we have a good day, we will arrive at the Vilaine."

"What is it like, the Vilaine?" asked Snowden. "I have seen the entrance to the estuary, it looked quite shallow. We would be very lucky to get to the shore, and to get a British ship to see us. Impossible, I would say."

"I am not a mariner, but I know quite large ships go in and out, but they are quite far from the land. The river itself goes a long way inland. It is …," he looked around, searching for the word, but giving up and indicating the rise and fall of the water with his hand.

"Tidal," said Snowden.

"Yes, exactly, tidal. When the tide is out it is very muddy. But Redon is a port, in good times quite busy."

"Should we go there?"

"I do not think so. The town has a garrison, and it is far from the sea. Tell me, Snowden, what you think we should do."

"I think we can't just stand on the shore at the mouth of the estuary. Even if we were lucky enough to see a British ship, it would be very hard to attract her attention without bringing attention to ourselves. Could we take a small boat? Perhaps, but we may have to go some distance at sea before we find a friendly ship. What I think we need is a reasonable-sized boat or ship that will take us down the river and well out to sea. Biggish fishing boat would do. What do you think, Wilson?"

"I agree with you, sir. We have to get well out to sea. I have to say, sir, I think it will be quite difficult to get a skipper to take us. I think we might have to indulge in a bit of cutting out."

"I think so too, Wilson."

Trezeguet nodded. "I think, Snowden, that we should make our way to a place on the north bank of the river, Foleux. Very lonely, but there is a jetty there, and if we are lucky there will be boats."

They set out early, but everyone in the party was very tired, and progress was much slower than it had been, the men seemingly interested only in the task in hand – putting one foot in front of the other. Snowden, exhausted, sometimes felt that he had been walking through Brittany for ever, and that his previous life, of ships, houses and indeed of being subordinate to some authority other than his own, was relegated to a dim memory.

Just after midday they stood at the summit of a gentle hill. Wilson spoke, "Sir, over there. Sky's got the look of the sea about it, if you know what I mean."

Snowden looked where he was pointing, and then at his compass. The sky was certainly bright in that direction.

"I see what you mean, Wilson. What do you think, Trezeguet?"

"It is the coast, without doubt, gentlemen."

Snowden looked at the men, who had been watching this exchange. They had been roused from their exhaustion, and were now talking animatedly among themselves, pointing at the sky towards the south-west. He turned to Wilson. "I think I'd better speak to them."

"Aye, sir."

The men formed a rough semicircle round Snowden.

"I know the last few days – seems like a lifetime – have been pretty hard. We won a victory, burning their barges, but we've lost some of our companions, left them behind. We've been through a great deal, and we're by no means through it yet, but there is hope. You can see the brightness in the sky over there. We all know what that means, the sea. It's Biscay, specifically Quiberon Bay. Many of you will have been there in ships, but I'll warrant none of you has walked there from the Channel before. It's been a long walk …."

"Walk!" one of the men whispered audibly, "run more like."

"Yes, Johnson, a bit of running as well, but the point is, we're nearly at the end of it. As I was saying, we can't just walk along the seashore and wave to a passing frigate. You know our ships keep well out to sea, and you know that Froggie keeps a good watch on Quiberon. We must get out to sea, to our fleet, and that means a boat."

There was some muttering from the men. Snowden realised that some of them had thought that standing on the seashore and waving was exactly what they would do.

"Ahead of us there's a river, the Vilaine. Some of you will have been in the estuary. Nasty place, shallow, full of sandbanks. Trezeguet here," Snowden pointed to the Breton, "knows a little port well up the river. Perhaps three leagues from here. Probably no Frenchies, but very likely some boats."

He paused, and looked at the men. "It's pretty simple. We go to this place, and take a boat or boats, and head down the river and out to sea. Once we get off the land, we can find an English ship."

There was a stirring from the men, and Snowden held up his hand. "I know, yes, I know it's not going to be easy, but we have no choice, and we have to do it quickly, or sure as can be Froggie will be after us. We've done some pretty good work, and with a bit more work and a dash of luck we'll soon be out of it. Jackson?"

He looked at one of the men, a young able seaman.

"Yes, sir."

"You were telling me about your grandfather the other evening, and the stories he told you."

"I was, sir. He was master's mate, in *La Magnanime*," he enunciated the name of the captured French 74 carefully, "with Hawke's squadron. At Quiberon Bay. They went right inshore, after a Frenchman. And before that they were giving Froggie what for in the Basque Roads. The tales he used to tell me, sir."

Snowden looked at Jackson, and then at the men. "Well, Jackson, you'll soon have a story of your own to rival your grandfather's. And that goes for all of you."

He turned to Wilson. "Let us proceed, Sergeant Wilson."

Chapter 31 – Awakening

Indescribable pain, lying on something hard. Darkness. A woman's touch, and then a voice, familiar.

"Jack."

I could not speak.

"Jack, you must be strong. The doctor is going to remove the ball."

Pain, excruciating, seeming to last for a long time. And then sleep, dream-filled delirious sleep. Nightmares, but sometimes it seemed as though the girl from Paris, Dominique, was there. And then, from time to time, a hand on my forehead, cool, and always gentle.

Nightmares, visions, but always that presence.

And then I awoke, and she was there. I searched for the French words: "I knew. I knew you were here."

I floated through the next few days in a haze of laudanum, something that I have come to despise, but Dominique was always close by, and we had wonderful talks.

One morning I felt her touch, and woke to see her by the bed, silhouetted by the light from the window. I could see immediately from her face that something was wrong, and when she told me of her father's wound, I felt truly sickened. We, the English had done that. We believed that we had no choice but to do it, and probably the French felt the same way. That war could do such things, not only to the men that fought in them, but also to their wives and daughters, was utterly repugnant to me, and I knew that I could have no more to do with it.

She was gone within the hour, on a canal boat, and I was left, devastated.

Despite my anguish, my body continued to mend, and before long I was able to get out of bed and spend time sitting in a chair. I had asked the doctor, Monsieur Quiniou, to stop dosing me with laudanum as I disliked the dreams that came with it, and from time to time the pain was often severe. I spoke to my fellow English patients sometimes, but I was not sociable and kept my own company as much as I could. They were worried about what would happen to them when they were no longer in hospital, but I could add nothing to their discussion.

About a week after Dominique had left, I heard a commotion outside the room, with Quiniou's voice raised in anger. "No, you cannot take him. He is weak, and the journey …."

He was interrupted by a rough voice. "We have our orders, doctor, directly from Monsieur Fouché, and I can assure you that there can be no arguing with his instructions. Kindly stand aside."

With sudden horror I remembered the name, and the man, and realised why the men were here. Fouché. Two men came into the room, large and unpleasant looking.

"Which one of you is Stone?"

There was silence in the room. I knew it was no good. They would find me.

"I am Stone. What do you want?"

"You are to come with us. You are arrested on a charge of theft."

Quiniou came into the room and interposed himself between me and the men. "Theft?" he asked, "What has he stolen?"

"A boat."

"Do not be ridiculous, he has stolen nothing. He is a British officer."

"He is a criminal, and he …."

The doctor stepped forwards, but the larger of the two men pushed him, hard, in the chest, and the elderly man fell backwards, striking his head on the edge of the door as he fell. He lay on the floor, breathing hard.

"Stay there, you bastard," said the man, and then to me, "Get up, now."

By now people had started to arrive from other parts of the building. Perhaps there were ten or so clustered around the door, some helping the doctor to his feet. One of them spoke, and by the adze in his hand, I judged his trade to be that of a carpenter.

"Why have you done this? The doctor is friend to all of us."

"He may be your friend, but he seems to me to be an enemy of the Republic. We have orders, from the very highest, to take this Englishman with us to Paris." He gestured towards me.

At this time, France, and especially Brittany, was a lawless place, much more unsettled than England. Paris was a long way away, and the people did not accept orders readily.

"Enemy of the Republic is he? And what has this Englishman done? I know what you people are like." The man started to raise his adze, and I saw with horror that the two men had drawn pistols.

"No," I shouted, as loudly as I could. "There is to be no fighting. I will go with them."

----------✳✳✳---------

The journey to Paris is something I will never forget, although I would dearly love to. I slumped in the corner of the carriage as it bumped and jolted. The contrast between this journey and my previous one with Snowden, when we had so happily and frivolously ridden to Paris on the horses Snowden had won, could not have been greater. The guards haphazardly administered the laudanum which the doctor had given them before we left, and this meant that for most of the time I floated on the boundary between consciousness and oblivion, often assailed by the most fantastic dreams. Sometimes I was dimly aware of changes of the horses, and occasionally the inside of coaching houses.

For two days we stayed at an inn somewhere on the road because my captors, the most horrible men I have met in my life, feared I might die unless I rested – a belief in which they were probably correct. This certainly had a beneficial effect on my health, although my spirits were very low.

Eventually we entered Paris, as I had done with Snowden, and through the same gate, but now there was no feeling of anticipation, only dread. I was a prisoner of Fouché, that evil man, and I was sure that there would be no escape. In the middle of Paris, the coach stopped in the courtyard of a tall building. Men in uniform – guards or soldiers – came out to meet the coach, and the brutes who had taken me in Brittany handed me over to them.

These men took me inside the building. I was able to walk, almost unaided, but my body was wracked with pain. Inside was a spacious room, and the guards halted me before a large table, encumbered by legers, at which sat a thin, elderly man flanked by two more guards.

"Monsieur Stone, I believe," he said, almost in the manner of an innkeeper greeting a guest. I felt a flicker of anger.

"You are mistaken, monsieur. I am not Monsieur, but rather Midshipman Stone, of His Britannic Majesty's Navy."

He blinked and spoke in an ingratiating manner. "Citizen Fouché has instructed me to take care of you. I believe you will not find our establishment wanting." He smiled at me.

"What is your establishment called?" I asked, knowing and dreading the answer.

"It is commonly known as the Temple, Monsieur Midshipman."

I could not help but shiver. The man smiled again, and spoke in the manner of a publican defending his establishment. "I see you have heard of this place. But you should know that we do not accommodate common criminals. Oh, no. Only gentlemen who have committed crimes of a political nature. Why, only yesterday, a thief, an ordinary thief, was escorted here. I had no hesitation, none whatsoever, in refusing to take the man. This place has a reputation."

Indeed it did, I thought.

"We have even accommodated royalty." He grabbed a thick ledger, thumbed through it rapidly, and turned it so that I could see the entries.

"Here, the late Louis and Madame Capet."

He saw my lack of recognition at the names.

"The *ci-devant* king and his wife, Marie Antoinette." He shuffled through the pages again. "And here, your very own Sidney Smith, an admiral I believe. And now we shall add your name to this famous list." He wrote, with a flourish, and gestured towards the book. "See, Monsieur Midshipman, you are amongst illustrious company. So young, and a guest of Citizen Fouché."

God preserve me, I thought.

The commandant nodded to the guards. "Close confinement."

The guards seized me by the elbows. If they had not, I do not believe that I would have been capable of movement. They half carried me up interminable flights of stone stairs, until one of them unlocked the door of a small room, with stone walls, barely furnished, a straw pallet against the wall. They turned and shut the door behind them, and I heard the grate of the key in the lock and the heavy footsteps of the men descending the stairs. I lay on the pallet and stared at the ceiling, despair rising in me. "Close confinement" was the evil-sounding phrase the commandant had used, made worse because I knew that I was in the Temple, that terrible prison where enemies of the state were held, and that Fouché, the wicked Minister of Police, had ordered my arrest.

I thought of Sidney Smith, whose entry in the leger the governor had showed me, and remembered what Snowden had told me about him. He had interfered with Bonaparte's plans, as I had, twice, and I was now paying the penalty. Smith had managed to escape somehow, but he had been the "Hero of Acre", an influential captain, a famous man, and unlike me a man of means and resources. The story of the other prisoners the governor had spoken of, the Famille Capet, had not ended happily.

In a miasma of unhappiness and terror, I slept.

Dominique had left Jack with a heavy heart, dreading what she would find at St Malo. By evening she was at her father's bedside in a beautiful room in a comfortable house with a large window looking out over the estuary. The barge that had brought her was still moored to the jetty at the end of the garden.

Her father, always so strong and vigorous, looked terrible. Pale, thin, weak. His hair was gone, as were his eyebrows. His shaved scalp revealed a terrible scar on the top of his head, a scar that had endlessly fascinated her when she was a little girl. She remembered how he would make up stories of how he had got the scar, usually involving mermaids and sea monsters.

She saw his eyes on her as she followed the doctor into the room.

"Dominique," he whispered.

"How are you, father?"

"I admit I have been better."

"What happened?"

"I cannot remember. I recollect nothing whatsoever from the time I left an inn with Bonaparte and Murat until the time I was on the quayside. Murat has told me that there was a fireship and we boarded it." Her father laughed weakly, "He may even be telling the truth."

The doctor, a youngish man, but thin and careworn, interjected. "The loss of memory is quite common in these situations. Sometimes it returns, but sometimes not."

Morlaix smiled slightly. "My leg, however, is certainly gone forever."

"Sadly, Citizen Morlaix, that it true."

Before she had entered the room, the doctor had told her that he had been forced to amputate her father's right leg just above the knee: "Unfortunately, Miss Morlaix, the leg was so badly damaged that there was no possibility of saving it."

Her father looked down, and winced. "It is gone, without doubt, but I can still feel it."

He spoke to the doctor. "Brabant, would you be so good as to allow me a private conversation with my daughter?"

"Of course, Citizen Morlaix. But do not exert yourself."

The doctor left the room, and her father rested back against his pillow. She felt so sorry for him, her indestructible father reduced to this pale shadow, with a framework keeping the covers from pressing on his leg, or at least the place where his leg used to be.

"Come and sit by me, Dominique. I feel very weak, but so much happier now you are here."

"I am very glad to be here, father, and sorry to see you in this condition. My god, how I hate the war." She felt herself to be very close to tears.

"My daughter, can you tell me what has happened to you?"

"Father, I can tell you that the barges were attacked by the English. Many of them are burned."

He winced. "I know, Dominique. The attack here, on St Malo, I believe it was a diversion. The real target was the barges, though I have no idea how the English knew they were there. I did not want to leave them undefended, but I could do nothing. It was all a waste."

Dominique felt tears run down her cheeks, and reached out to put her hand on her father's arm.

"That is enough, father. We should not dwell on it."

"Were you clear of the fighting, Dominique?"

"Yes, Peress and I hid in the house. We were nowhere near it, though we did see the English as they retreated."

"And then …?"

Dominque realised that the lieutenant who had brought the news of the barges to her father had also given him an account of her activities.

"I helped Monsieur Quiniou with the wounded."

"So I have heard. It is said that you and he did a wonderful job. He is a good man, I knew him in Toulon." His voice was becoming very weak.

"I believe you should sleep now, father. I will be here to help from now on."

His eyes were already closed.

When Madame Morlaix arrived from Paris a few days later, her husband was sleeping less, but still very weak. It was another month before it was decided that he could be moved back to Paris. He was laid on an improvised bed in the carriage, and each day the family travelled for a few hours only.

Snowden suddenly felt a fierce pride in his men, ordinary men who were making the best of a truly extraordinary situation, and an overwhelming sense of responsibility for them. He would do it, get them out, and in the process add to the store of tales they would be able to tell their grandchildren.

"Wilson, now seems to be a good time to rest the men. If you please, get them into the wood over there. Set pickets, but two hours' rest."

"Aye aye, sir."

"I'm going forward with Trezeguet to have a look from the top of that hill in front of us. Trezeguet, with me please."

Snowden and Trezeguet set out along the road, which dipped and then climbed up a hill, gentle in slope, but higher than the one on which they had left the men. The view from the top of the hill was obscured by a stand of trees. He looked at the largest tree, a chestnut.

"Trezeguet, I'm going up this tree for a look round. A leg up, if you'd be so good."

With the Breton's help, Snowden reached the lower branch, swung himself up and climbed steadily. When the branches were too thin to support him, he stopped. He had chosen well, and the tree was higher than the others round it, and as he looked, he felt a rush of excitement. Ahead, snaking through a sparsely populated countryside, was a river, or at least the muddy bed of what would be a river when the tide was high. On the left, in the distance, Snowden could see the spires and buildings of a substantial town, and with a start he realised that the masts and rigging of ships were visible, presumably alongside a wharf. He looked at his compass, making a mental note of the bearing of the town and the furthest bend of the river that he could see.

Resisting the urge to rush, he climbed down, dropping to the ground near Trezeguet, and set his compass level on the ground. He sighted along it, and pointed with his hand.   "Over there, Trezeguet, perhaps two leagues distant, there's a substantial town. Church spires, big buildings. Ships alongside a wharf." He swept his hand round, from left to right. "And along there, a river. The tide is low, and there is hardly any water in it at the moment. It disappears around a bend, and that is all I can see of it."

Trezeguet smiled. "Without doubt, Snowden, the town over there is Redon, and the river is the Vilaine. Two leagues, you say?"

"I believe so, yes."

"Well, our destination, Foleux, should be, let me see, about in that direction." Trezeguet pointed, and Snowden sighted along the compass, noting the bearing the Breton was indicating. "Perhaps three leagues."

Snowden thought, calculating, thinking of the phase of the moon, and took out his pocket watch. "I don't know exactly, Trezeguet, but I think that the tide is probably dead low presently. Let us get to this Foleux as soon as we can, and see what is there."

They returned to the place where the rest of the party was hidden, and Snowden spoke to Wilson. "Went up a tree on the hill over there, Wilson. Stiffish climb, no ratlines, and no lubber hole either."

Wilson smiled at the reference to the rigging of a ship. "Anything visible from the foretop, sir?"

"Yes, Wilson, by God there was. I saw the river, the Vilaine, running through the country. Tide's out, so it's just mud at the moment. I reckon it's dead low. And there's a town, quite a substantial place over there," he pointed, "two leagues or so away. There are ships there, too, alongside a wharf I reckon."

Wilson nodded, his eyes alight.

"This place, Foleux, which Trezeguet is keen, on. Little place he says, with an inn and a small wharf, is a three of leagues over there." Snowden pointed again. "We'll go there directly, and see what we can find. If there's something there that can carry all of us, we stand a chance of getting out tonight on the tide. I reckon it'll be high about three in the morning. There must be the devil of a current on the ebb."

At about nine in the evening, they arrived in the vicinity of Foleux, after a tense and tiring march, avoiding villages along the way by taking long detours across the fields. The men concealed themselves in a wood, from which they could see the river, becoming fuller as the tide rose.

Snowden spoke: "I'm going with Trezeguet, Wilson. We'll just have a look at the place and see if there's anything useful to us there."

"Useful, sir?"

"I mean a ship or boat, Wilson. Have two of the men follow behind us, to keep an eye on things. And, if you please, make sure the men here stay alert. We may have to move quickly."

"Aye, sir, I'll do that."

Snowden and Trezeguet walked cautiously along the white road in the gathering dusk, the air full of insects and heavy with the smell of wild flowers. After a hundred yards or so they came to a small cottage, dark within and seemingly unoccupied, and then to a few others, some with dim lights inside. Suddenly, Trezeguet stopped and pulled Snowden back by the shoulder.

"Over there," he whispered, pointing.

With a start, Snowden saw the river, a small jetty protruding into it from the bank. At the end of the jetty, clearly aground and leaning against the piling, Snowden saw a ketch of perhaps fifty tons.

"By God, Trezeguet, she would do very nicely."

They moved forward along the road. Ahead, opposite the jetty, was a lighted building, from which came the sounds of music and laughter. Occasionally the shadows of dancers could be seen on the windows. Momentarily, Snowden allowed himself to imagine that he was inside the inn, snug and secure.

As they moved towards the jetty, Snowden could see that the ketch needed perhaps a foot more of water before she would float, and, judging by the way the flood tide was running, he thought that would be in an hour or so.

The wind, quite a fresh breeze, appeared to be from the east, but Snowden knew that in rivers such as the Vilaine the wind tended to blow along the river. He looked intently at the clouds.

"South-easterly," he said to himself.

"What?"

"Thinking out loud about the wind, Trezeguet. It seems to be south-easterly."

As they stepped out onto the narrow jetty, Snowden was absorbed by thoughts of the ship and the state of the tide, and his mind, dulled by fatigue and the relief of possible salvation, drew no inferences from the momentary increase in sound from the inn behind them.

Trezeguet, however, was sharper, and grabbed Snowden's sleeve. They turned to see a party of what were obviously mariners, led by a bearded man of sixty or so, advancing towards them and blocking the exit from the jetty.

The ship's crew, thought Snowden, with the master in front.

As the men advanced, Snowden and Trezeguet instinctively stepped backwards, further onto the jetty. The men stopped, and the master spoke rapidly in Breton. Trezeguet listened, held up his hand, and then spoke to Snowden.

"He wants to know who we are, and why we are interested in his ship. He does not think you are a French officer."

Snowden instinctively put his hand on the pistol in his belt, more to reassure himself that it was there than as an aggressive act, but two of the men leapt towards him and one of them struck him a tremendous blow with his fist on the side of his head, knocking him to the ground. His vision went black for an instant, and he felt his arms tied roughly behind his back.

As Snowden was being pulled to his feet, Trezeguet threw back his head and let out a screech, like that made by an owl, but much louder. The call of the Chouan, Snowden knew, and their captors reacted by moving away from Trezeguet, to what looked like a respectful distance, taking Snowden with them, and started talking among themselves. Snowden felt his captors' grip slackening.

The master went up to Trezeguet and a conversation ensued. After a while, the men shook hands, and as Snowden felt his arms being untied, Trezeguet turned to him. "I am sorry to startle you, Snowden, but the men here recognise the call of the Chouan very well."

"It is enough to startle one."

"The captain, he wishes to speak to you."

"Of course." Snowden winced. "I've been introduced to his crew already, so I may as well meet the man in charge."

The master joined them and shook hands with Snowden. To Snowden's surprise he spoke in English with what seemed to Snowden to be an American accent.

"Captain Berthou, at your service."

"Snowden, Lieutenant, Royal Navy, likewise. You speak English."

"I knew you were English Navy by 'the cut of your jib'. Yes, twenty years trading in America. Now, your English ships are everywhere and the trade is finished. I have now only a very small ship, to evade the blockade you understand, but even so she has been lying here for a month."

From the corner of his eye, Snowden saw movement on the road. He forced his eyes away and spoke to the captain, wondering how he could play his hand.

"I will speak frankly with you, Berthou."

Berthou nodded.

"I am badly in need of either a ship or passage in one. In yours, for example."

"In my ship?"

Snowden allowed himself to look towards the road and saw Wilson at the head of the men, walking softly, but in a formation that Snowden hoped was good enough to look intimidating.

Snowden held up his hand, and Wilson saw the gesture and the men halted, between the group on the jetty and the inn, their bayonets fixed on their sloped muskets.

Berthou and his crew noticed the men, and there was silence as the English party formed into two lines – the forward one kneeling with their muskets beside them, and the rear one standing behind them, vertical, with the butts resting on the ground. The bayonets glinted in the light from the inn.

Snowden gestured to the men, put his hand on the pistol in his belt, and spoke to Berthou.

"My sergeant has a flair for the dramatic, but I will take passage in your ship, one way or another. I have some gold with me." Snowden extracted the money pouch, still heavy with gold, from his coat, and patted it. At that time, in France, gold was scarce. "And future arrangements will depend on you."

Berthou looked at the bag and nodded. "My ship is valuable, worth more than the gold you have there."

"That may be so, but I will have her. I can take her if I wish," Snowden gestured towards the men with their muskets, "with no gold changing hands."

A cunning look came over Berthou's face, and he shook his head. "You will never navigate the mouth of the Vilaine."

"It would certainly be easier with the assistance of a pilot, which is why I would prefer an amicable arrangement."

Snowden noticed the door of the inn open. People came through to stand outside, and he shouted to Wilson, "Those people are to go back inside, Wilson, and send a couple of men to stop anyone getting out of the back."

"Aye, sir. Are we to have the ship?"

"Yes, we are to have her."

"Berthou, I believe that you will fit the bill for a pilot exactly, so shall we say that we would like to take passage on your ship? We will agree a sum, and I will personally see that you are paid as soon as you deliver us. A commercial transaction, nothing more."

"You know that it is more than that. I will not be able to return. A Breton, transporting the enemy. I will not be welcome."

"Indeed you may not, but I have no doubt that the British Navy can give your ship full employment. Your cargo?"

"Grain."

"I am sure that there would be a market for grain in England."

"No doubt. I seem to have no choice. My wife is aboard the ship. She will come with me."

Snowden relaxed, the hand had been played.

"The ship is afloat, we will depart immediately."

Snowden called Trezeguet over and beckoned for Wilson to join them. "We seem to have passage on this fine vessel, which is just about to float, so we must act quickly. The captain here will pilot us through the estuary."

"Trezeguet, take this gold and give each of the crew that will swear they will not raise the alarm a piece. If any so wish, they may come with us. Wilson, put the rest of the crew inside the inn and block the doors."

Trezeguet and Wilson moved over to the group of Breton seamen.

Snowden and Berthou, with three of the English sailors, walked down the jetty and stepped onto the deck of the ship. By now it was quite dark, but Snowden thought the ship seemed well found. Berthou went into the cabin, and Snowden heard a subdued conversation between him and his wife.

They got a foresail hoisted, and let its sheets fly so that it cracked in the breeze. There was a rush of feet on the jetty, as men flung themselves over the bulwarks onto the deck. Wilson shouted, "Form up, muster."

When he was sure that the men were all accounted for, Wilson turned to Snowden. "All present, sir."

Men moved to the mooring lines. Snowden said, "Let go fore and aft."

The lines splashed into the river. Men ran on the deck, sheeting in the foresail. It cracked once, and then drew, pulling the ship forward. Snowden turned to Berthou at the helm.

"You have the ship, Captain."

The ketch stemmed the tide, and moved slowly away from the jetty.

Light streamed from the windows of the inn ashore, but on the ship it was completely dark. Snowden had studied hard for his lieutenant's examination, and he had retained a good understanding of the working of the tides. He thought hard: "*Moon was full six days ago. High water Dover at full moon, midday; Brest low when Dover high ....*"

He spoke to the ship's master at the helm, his eyes on the outline of the hills bordering the river, which were silhouetted against the slightly lighter sky.

"High about midnight, I calculate."

Berthou kept his eyes on the ship's heading. "Yes, Lieutenant. But neaps now, the flood is not very strong."

"Will there be enough water in the entrance?"

"There will, Lieutenant, but it will be difficult in the dark."

"Should be a bit of moon by then."

"There should, but even so, it is a difficult place."

"Shall we get some sail on her?"

"We should. She will stand all of the canvas tonight."

"I will see to it." Snowden moved forward. It felt very good, almost like coming home, to feel the way of the ship beneath him. He could dimly make out the men, who were mostly sitting on the hatch coaming.

"Well done, men, we're on our way now."

One of the men spoke. In the darkness, Snowden could not make out who it was. "Will they come after us, sir?"

"I don't know. There is a garrison at Redon, but that's inland, so they won't be able to catch us if somebody rouses them. I don't know what is further down the river. We'll have to take our chance. We'll have the mainsail on her now. Two men aft to take care of the sheet, rest of you on the halyards."

Ten minutes later, the ship, which Snowden learned was called *Penfret*, was sailing quickly with the wind on the quarter, the dimly visible banks of the river, high against the sky, seeming to rush past. Berthou steered the ship round a bend, and the lights of the inn disappeared behind them.

Snowden called out softly, "Trezeguet, Wilson, come aft to the helm if you please."

He heard movement forward, and the Breton and the sergeant joined him near the helm.

Snowden spoke so Berthou could hear: "Berthou, do you know if there are any soldiers ashore, or guard boats in the river between us and the sea?"

"I do not know. Sometimes there are boats with soldiers at Roche Bernard."

Snowden had not heard of Roche Bernard. "How far is this place?"

"Perhaps a league from here."

"We will be up with it shortly then?"

"Yes."

Snowden spoke to the sergeant: "Wilson, have the men at the bulwarks, lying down out of sight. Load and fix bayonets to repel boarders, but be sure not to fire unless I give the order. Jackson and Andrews, in the bows if you please, a good lookout."

"Aye aye, sir."

"Trezeguet, stay here at the helm with Berthou. We may need to converse with a guard boat."

Snowden was sure that the Chouan would understand that he wanted an eye kept on the ship's master. Snowden thought that the likelihood of treachery was not great, as any betrayal would leave Berthou exposed to retaliation from the French. For good or worse, he felt Berthou was committed to them now.

"I think we must decide on a story."

Berthou spoke: "If challenged, I will say that we are bound for Auray, and we are trying to get across the Bay of Quiberon in the darkness, in case the English are inshore."

Snowden considered. It seemed reasonable to him. "What do you think, Trezeguet?"

"I think it is a story as good as any. It may pass muster. Let us hope there is no guard boat."

At that moment, the cabin door opened and the figure of a woman could be dimly made out. Madame Berthou, Snowden assumed. She spoke in Breton to her husband, and went back down the companionway.

The river seemed to grow narrower, and the banks higher. Snowden thought they would probably look like cliffs in daylight. There was a soft hail from the bows: "Shore lights on the port bow, high up."

Berthou spoke from the helm: "Roche Bernard."

The voice from the bows replied: "Red light, if you please, on a boat in the river, I reckon."

"I see it. The guard boat." Snowden's heart beat quickly. "They may not see us. Their lamp is bright. I will hug the right bank, away from the town."

The ship was travelling fast, her sails straining. Snowden realised that Berthou was trying to make sure that the ship was not silhouetted against the shore lights. The ship was opposite what Snowden could see was a small port, with lighted buildings surrounding it. Behind them, apparently at great height, were the lights of a town. The boat with the red lantern was on the port bow, perhaps a cable's length away.

The ship rushed through the night. The shape of the guard boat could now be seen, illuminated by its lantern. Snowden tensed as the ship quickly drew level with the boat and then left it astern. Snowden began to relax, and then worried that the men in the boat would notice the waves of the ship's wash. Suddenly, almost simultaneously, several things happened.

A cry from the lookout: "Ship dead ahead!"

Berthou put the helm up suddenly. As the ship answered, there was an impact, which threw Snowden to the deck. *Penfret* heeled violently, accompanied by a horrible grinding noise and the smashing of timber, as she slid along the side of what Snowden believed to be a large ship, though he had no more than a vague impression of a black bulk. And then *Penfret* was free, sailing as quickly as before.

Snowden ran forward. "Is anybody injured?"

"I don't believe so, sir, though the bulwark's stove in on the starboard bow," replied Jackson.

Andrews added, "I saw her just before we hit, anchored in the stream she was, no lights at all. Reckon she might have been a sloop o' war, sir, laid up."

"Very well, keep your eyes skinned, we don't want any more surprises. Lucky we didn't have the sticks out of her." From astern, he could hear the sound of shouting, and saw the waving of lanterns. They're too late, Snowden thought, *Penfret* would be at the entrance before the French realised what had happened.

They were kept busy, working the ship as she followed the bends in the river, but soon the tide turned in their favour and their progress became very rapid. A weak moon rose behind them, revealing low banks on either side as the river widened.

Madame Berthou came on deck and distributed bread and cider to the men. Snowden ate, and felt immensely refreshed. They passed what seemed to be a village, and then another, and then as the river gave way to a wide estuary, Snowden felt the ship lift to what was unmistakably the remnant of an ocean swell.

Berthou steered with great concentration and occasionally gave orders to the men. "Depth, if you please," he shouted. There was cursing from the chains.

"By the mark four, far as I can tell, but she's going devilish fast for lead work."

"Thank you."

The sound of cannon fire came from far away. Probably the ship they had collided with, Snowden thought. He realised that he had been so focused on immediate problems that he had given little thought as to how they would make their escape once they were at sea.

Berthou spoke to Snowden, his face pale in the moonlight. "Those guns, they are raising the alarm."

Snowden had come to the same conclusion. "Will it do them any good?"

"It depends. I do not know if they have any ships at the entrance. Perhaps not, as your Navy sometimes ventures very close inshore." Berthou made a small alteration of course and shouted, "Watch that outer jib sheet."

"Aye aye" came from forward.

He spoke again to Snowden: "I believe that there are galleys based on the Ile du Met. I expect they will hear the guns and perhaps put to sea. We will give the island a wide berth, but there is not much room. The tide is falling, and to go aground …."

He did not finish, but Snowden knew that the ship aground would be an easy target for the French. They sailed on for an hour, without incident, the ship pitching in the swell. The Biscay swell, thought Snowden. With any luck, they would get clear now. There was a cry from a lookout forward. "Land on the port bow, four points. Low, looks like an island."

"Ile du Met," said Berthou.

Snowden made his way forward to the lookouts in the bows. "Where away?"

The lookout pointed. "There, sir."

Snowden looked in the direction of the man's pointing hand. "I see it."

A small, low island was just visible. It was difficult to make out any detail, but he had the impression that there were buildings on it. He returned aft and spoke to Berthou, and told him what he had seen.

"What will we do now?"

Berthou thought for a moment. "I believe it will be best for us to stand on for perhaps an hour, until the island is on the quarter, and then wear her round and stand out to sea."

Snowden remembered the island-strewn coastline of the Bay of Quiberon, and thought that standing out to sea had its attractions.

"I agree, Berthou, we should get as much offing as we can before it gets light."

The ship rushed on through the night, the island gradually changing its bearing, abeam and then on the quarter.

There was a cry from the lookout. "Land dead ahead."

"That is Ile Hoëdic," said Berthou. "I believe we should wear the ship round now."

"I agree. Shall we light the binnacle first?"

The binnacle lamp was lit, and Snowden could see by the compass that the course was south-west. He tried to visualise the chart as the ship was gybed and headed due south. There was a call from the lookout. "Boat ahead, two points on the port bow. Very close."

Berthou put the helm down, and Snowden shouted, "Sheets there."

The men hardened in the sails, and the ship heeled as she came onto the wind. Snowden made his way forward. The lookout did not have to point. Illuminated by the weak moonlight, there was a boat ahead, close. A large boat, with perhaps twenty oarsmen. He saw the boat turn towards them, and men clamber over the oarsmen to the swivel mounted on her bow. He shouted, "Down, behind the bulwarks!" as the men at the swivel pointed the weapon towards the ship.

The swivel fired, its flash blinding in the darkness, sending grapeshot screaming across the narrow gap between the two vessels, most of it whistling over the deck, but he heard thuds as some of it hit the ship. There was a crash from above, and Snowden looked up to see the peak of the mainsail gaff fall in a tangle of rope, bringing the topsail with it. Got the peak halyard, thought Snowden. Lucky shot.

The ship came upright, slowing. Snowden cursed. He saw men in the boat busy with rope and grapnel, while others struggled to reload the swivel.

"Stand by to repel boarders," he shouted, as the grapnel hooked over the port bulwark, and the boat was dragged along by the ship, crashing alongside amidships, water foaming at her bow. The men stood up, holding their muskets with fixed bayonets, and Snowden rushed aft along the deck, drawing his pistol. The swivel fired again, so close to him that he felt the heat from its muzzle. He felt a sharp pain in his ears, and from that moment on the rest of the action seemed to be silent, save for the sound of his own voice.

He stopped at the grapnel which was firmly wedged in between the capping of the bulwark and the mainmast lanyards, the rope tight with the weight of the boat dragged along by the ship. He pulled at it without effect, but almost instantly his efforts were assisted by crewmen who came to his aid. He looked up and saw Frenchmen stand up in the boat and grasping the bulwarks of the ship. He felt elation surge through him and shouted, "Boarders!"

He left the men struggling with the grapnel and launched himself along the deck towards the boarders. The first man was just over the bulwark, starting to stand upright with a cutlass in his hand, when Snowden was upon him, clubbing him brutally with the pistol in his hand. As the man dropped onto the deck, Snowden went for the second man, who seemed to be having second thoughts. The English seamen had managed to free the grapnel, the towrope had gone slack, and the gap between ship and boat was starting to widen. The man saw Snowden running towards him, and without ceremony jumped over the bulwark into the boat. Snowden saw the boat dropping back and men working on the swivel. He shouted, "Down!"

The swivel fired, but the men were safely behind the bulwarks, and there were no more crashes from the rigging. *Penfret* surged on, much faster in the rising gale than the galley, despite her scandalised mainsail and wrecked topsail. He went aft. Berthou was at the helm, apparently unperturbed. He said something, but Snowden, out of breath from the exertion, shook his head, pointing to his ears. The ship sailed on, south, and then south-west. They saw no ships, not even a fishing boat.

By the time dawn came, red and angry-looking, *Penfret* was far out to sea, sailing fast, well reefed down, in a strong south-westerly gale, which continued to rise as the morning went on.

Just before midday they hove the ship to, and she lay easily with the wind just forward of the beam, though spray drove across the decks. Occasionlly a breaking crest would hit the ship, and she would shudder, as water foamed across the decks.

As night fell, Berthou and Snowden were in the ship's cabin, leaning across the table on which the chart was spread. Snowden spoke to Berthou above the noise of the wind in the rigging, pointing at a spot on the chart with the point of the dividers.

"About there, I believe."

"I think that is about right, say twenty leagues south-west of the Saintes." The Saintes were islands stretching out into the Atlantic from the coast of Brittany.

Snowden gripped the table tightly as the ship was struck by a wave crest, its hissing clearly heard in the cabin. A heavy blow, thought Snowden, but perhaps not as strong as the ones the ship had encountered during the afternoon. He glanced at the French officer, grey and ill looking, his head bandaged, sleeping heavily on the settee at the side of the cabin.

"Is the wind going down now, Berthou?"

"I believe it is, Snowden."

Snowden pointed at the chart. "It may veer round to the north-west soon. If it does, we'll more or less be on a lee shore. Quite a bit of searoom, but we'd be better off keeping well out to sea."

Berthou nodded his agreement.

"Do you think we could get her underway? If we could make use of this south-westerly, perhaps we could get past Ushant, and then if the wind veered it would be a fair breeze."

"This is a good scheme. Let us leave it for a little while, and see if it really is moderating."

Half an hour later they went on deck. Snowden spoke to the man in the cockpit, who was watching the lashed helm.

"What's it doing, Davis?"

"I believe it's going down a bit, sir."

"Very well."

Snowden looked at Berthou, questioningly.

"I think we should, Snowden. We must never waste a fair wind. Please call the hands."

The men emerged from the fo'c'stle, their coats soon wet with spray, and Snowden arranged them on the staysail sheets. Berthou and Davis removed the lashing from the helm. The men, shivering in their wet clothes, crouched ready. Berthou nodded to Snowden who shouted, "Weather foremast staysail sheet, let fly." And then, "Lee sheet, harden in."

The staysail cracked loudly in the wind, and men tramped along the deck, sheeting in the sail, which began to draw. The ship slowly forged ahead, her head starting to move up into the wind. Berthou, assisted by Davis, put the helm up, and Snowden shouted again, "Slacken away on the mainsheet."

The mainboom swung out, and the mainsail flapped slowly and violently, shaking the mast and the ship, but *Penfret*, under the combined influence of rudder and staysail, began to turn away from the wind.

Snowden looked at Berthou, who held up his hand, mouthing "Wait." When the ship was broadside on to the wind Berthou nodded, and Snowden ordered, "Harden in the main."

The ship heeled and began to move, slowly at first, but gathering speed in the gale until she was rushing through the night, on a north-westerly course, out into the Atlantic.

Snowden looked anxiously up at the straining sails and rigging, and then at Berthou.

"Do not worry, Snowden, she is sound. See how she runs!"

And indeed, Snowden had to admit, the ship was running wonderfully well, seeming to revel in the gale behind her. By the time the dawn broke, revealing a stark line of cloud with clear sky behind it, and the wind veered to the north, *Penfret* had run eighty miles or more, and was well clear of the vicious rocks and surging tides of the Breton coast. In the cabin, Snowden, Trezeguet, Berthou and Madame Berthou sat at the table.

Snowden looked at Berthou. "I believe we have no option but to head for St Peter's. My ship is based there, and I must report to the Admiral, Sausmarez. Trezeguet lives there, and I believe that Sausmarez will treat you fairly. The ship is not a prize, and we shall pay for our passage."

Trezeguet, who was an unenthusiastic seaman, looked unhappily at Snowden and groaned, "Sausmarez is a fine man, Berthou. He will do the right thing," before staggering over to the berth unoccupied by the French officer, where he lay back, apparently indifferent to further conversation.

Berthou looked at his wife, who reached across and squeezed his hand. There was a brief conversation in Breton.

"We are in your hands. Let it be Guernsey."

At the chart on the table, Snowden laid off the course and looked up at Berthou, whose face showed the strain of the last few days.

"Berthou, I will take the ship now. Please rest. You will need your wits about you when we get to Guernsey."

They anchored in the roadstead of St Peter's at ten the following morning, the black-and-white Breton flag at the mizzen peak, and Snowden watched as the admiral's barge put off from the jetty.

I played the cards as well as I could, he thought to himself, and perhaps I have won, but a price has been paid.

Chapter 35 – The Temple

I cannot bring myself to relate much about my time in the tower of the Temple. I believe that it is impossible to be terrified for long periods of time, and eventually my terror changed into something like a dull ache, always present, infinitely wearying. This, added to the physical pain of my wound, made me a prey to melancholy.

It was true that the guards were an improvement on the ones who had taken me in Brittany, but that was rather a low bar to surmount. My lack of money was clearly a disappointment to them, but they were not brutal, though rather uncommunicative. I had no contact with any other prisoners, but I could often hear people talking nearby, and sometimes shouting. From time to time I was allowed to exercise, not in the yard or the adjacent garden, but on a walkway on the roof, which led around the central tower. The walkway was surrounded by battlements, with shutters in the embrasures, rather ill fitting, and by putting my eye to the gaps I could look down on the bustling streets of Paris. I believe that without those glimpses of the world outside my prison I would have entirely lost the will to live.

The days turned to weeks. My wound continued to be very painful, and my spirits to decline. I spent increasing intervals on my pallet, and my appetite diminished so that I often did not eat the sparse meals provided to me. I began to think that I had been forgotten, and that I would die in the Temple.

One evening I heard the spy hatch in the door of my room open, and I looked up to see a pair of eyes fixed on me as I lay on my mattress. I could not bear to look in the direction of the door, and turned my head and looked at the wall. It seemed like a very long time until I heard the hatch scrape back. I was expecting the door to open and the owner of the eyes to visit me, but I heard footsteps retreating on the stone floor outside, and I was heartily relieved.

Later, the guard came into my room to deliver my meal.

"A visitor?"

"Yes, you are privileged. Citizen Fouché himself looked into your room."

"Why?"

"I do not know. He visited the Governor, and then asked to see you."

I felt a wave of dread pass over me.

The next few days were terrible. I ate almost nothing, I shivered constantly though the room was not cold, my wound throbbed, my dreams were vivid and horrible, and I hardly moved from my berth. I was almost wishing that Fouché would send for me; I felt that nothing could be worse than imprisonment without end in this terrible place.

One morning, I was lying on my bed, perhaps more than half asleep, after a dreadful night of wakefulness and nightmare, when I heard the key turn in the lock and the bolts drawn back. I was so borne down by misery and pain that I scarce had the energy to turn my head towards the door. I heard the guard's heavy footsteps, and felt him prod my shoulder.

"On your feet – visitor."

I did not react, and he grabbed my shoulder, fortunately my uninjured one, and pulled me round to face the door. Framed by the dark stone of the door aperture, so out of place in that horrible prison that I doubted my eyes, was a vision of hope and loveliness, as there stood Dominique, basket in hand, the Governor hovering anxiously behind her.

The day after Dominique, with her mother and father, arrived in Paris, visitors started to appear at the house. Her mother kept them downstairs, explaining that Morlaix was too ill to receive visitors, and accepting their cards and condolences. The visitors seemed happy to accept this, perhaps not really relishing time with a man who, it seemed, had been cut down in his prime.

It was about three in the afternoon when Dominique, who had been sitting beside her father, heard a knock at the door and looked up to see her mother with Talleyrand. She saw her father smile.

"Minister, it is good to see you."

"It is good to see you as well, Breton, but I am sorry that you are in this condition."

Morlaix spread his hands in an accepting gesture. "The fortunes of war, I suppose."

"Perhaps so, but I am here to deliver the sympathies of our First Consul."

"That is kind of him."

"Uncharacteristically so, but I believe that there was something approaching contrition in his demeanour when he asked me if I was to visit you."

"That would be a first."

"Indeed it would, perhaps I was mistaken..."

At the end of the visit, which seemed to boost her father's morale considerably, Dominique accompanied Talleyrand downstairs. To her surprise, as Talleyrand took his hat from a maid, he held Dominique by the arm and spoke softly into her ear, "Dominique, I heard what happened after the barges were attacked. I believe that you acted in an exemplary fashion, and I would have expected no less."

"Thank you, sir."

"The world knows that I am the most cynical of men."

"I'm sure it does not ..."

Talleyrand waved dismissively. "Be that as it may, I have a great affection for your father, and I would not like to see him, or his daughter, hurt."

"I do not see how we could be hurt."

"My correspondents inform me that you have formed an affection for one Midshipman Stone, of the British Navy, and that you nursed him after he was wounded in the attack."

Dominique thought that Talleyrand was indeed well informed, and felt a jolt of alarm.

"Jack – do you have news from Brittany? Is he well?"

"Dominique, the news I have for you is not from Brittany, but rather from Paris."

"I do not understand, please explain."

"I am afraid, Dominique, that the Midshipman was brought to Paris on the orders of Fouché, and is being held in close confinement in the Temple."

Dominique felt as though the floor had sloped beneath her.

"Why, what is he to Fouché? How can Jack be of interest to that …."

Talleyrand interrupted, "Have you ever asked Midshipman Stone why he left your mother's house so precipitately on the evening that he was there with Lieutenant … yes, Lieutenant Snowden?"

"No, I have never asked him, but I know why. My father told me. Fouché."

Suddenly, the pieces came together, and it seemed as though Dominique's entire world was crumbling. She leaned on the wall.

"Fouché had him arrested in Brittany and brought to the Temple," continued Talleyrand.

"But he was hardly well enough to be moved."

"I know, and I have been informed from persons privy to the situation that his condition there is not good. I am telling you this, Dominique, because Fouché's star is not as ascendant as it used to be, and the First Consul is under some obligation to your father. He would, for example, not wish your mother to whisper against him at her soirees."

Dominique was young, and her father did not think her cynical, but she realised that Talleyrand was bartering with her, or was bartering with her parents, with Dominique as the intermediary. His intentions may have been good, but he was nevertheless bartering.

"I understand, sir."

"Very well, Dominique. Should you wish to visit the Midshipman, I believe that you will find the governor amenable. I wish you good day, and please look after your father. The Republic cannot afford to lose men such as he."

---------✱✱✱---------

An hour later, Dominique, accompanied by a servant, a former coxswain of her father, was at the Temple. She knew of its reputation, made worse by the rumours that circulated about the horrible death of the son of "Louis and Marie Capet", the dauphine, and her fears grew for Jack as she awaited the arrival of the governor. He had clearly been forewarned of her visit, and took her personally up the long flights of stairs.

The guard accompanying them opened the door, and there was Jack, recognisably Jack, but so thin, and so languorous, lying on a pitiful bed on the floor. He did not turn at the opening of the door, but did not resist when the guard went forward and rather roughly turned him towards them. His eyes opened fully, and he stared at her.

"Dominique, is that really you?"

He struggled to his feet as Dominque embraced him, feeling his bones prominent through his shirt.

"It certainly is, Jack."

"It is so good to see you, Dominique."

"I have brought you some things. Shall we sit at the table?"

She helped him to the table, and they sat beside each other. She took bread and butter from her basket and set them before him.

"Jack, you are so thin. You should eat."

"I should, I know. They have been feeding me, but, well, I just have not felt hungry. My spirits were so low. They will never let me out of here. Fouché …." His voice trailed off, and his head dropped forwards nearly to his chest. Dominique brushed back the tears that had started from her eyes, dipped the bread in wine and held it to his mouth.

"Jack, please eat. There is hope. You are not forgotten."

Jack chewed at the bread, remembering. "Your father, how is he? Is he still in St Malo?"

"He is here, in Paris, at our house. He has lost his leg, but is recovering."

"My God, how terrible the war is."

She had left him asleep on his mattress, but though she knew that her presence had comforted him, she was desperately worried by his weakness, both physically and of spirit.

The house seemed weighed down by sorrow, and though Odile Morlaix did her best to spread a cheerfulness which she did not herself feel, the days dragged interminably.

Her husband, that vigorous and healthy man, was a shadow of his former self, lying in bed or sometimes sitting immobile in a chair, feeling pain in a leg that was no longer there. He spoke little, but spent nearly all day looking out of the tall window in his room, but without seeing much. The doctors spoke of a lengthy recovery, not only from the amputation, but also from the blow to his head and the subsequent lengthy unconsciousness. Though she did socialise occasionally, it was more out of habit than in the pursuit of pleasure, and perhaps, she thought to herself, to avoid the possibility of being forgotten, for the world to move forward without her. She felt that if it was not for Dominique, and her Jack (Odile smiled briefly as she realised that she was beginning to think of an Englishman, an enemy, as Jack, a person in his own right), she might well have taken her husband away from Paris, and let the politics be damned.

Dominique was very resistant to being cheered. She had returned from her first visit to Jack in reasonably good spirits, but after a week or more of daily visits to the Temple, her mood had darkened. Dominique was desperately worried about Jack, a worry that had spread to Odile.

Mother and daughter sat at the table in her husband's room, which, despite its light décor, was made gloomy by the immobile man sitting in the chair, uncommunicative, the stump of his missing leg propped up on a stool. Dominique had just returned from a visit to the Temple, and tears were rolling down her cheeks.

"Mother, I am terrified for Jack. He is so passive. When we were in Brittany, after he was wounded, we had such wonderful conversations, but now he hardly speaks, and I find the visits so difficult."

"I know that it must be very hard for you, but Jack will recover, just as your father will." Odile felt herself very close to tears, and reached out and took Dominique's hand.

"His spirit seems so crushed, mother, I do not believe that he will recover in that cursed place. And it is not just his spirit, his wounds give terrible pain."

"My dear, I do not know what to say …."

"I know what to say."

They both turned in surprise as Morlaix spoke, more forcefully than he had done since his injury. His face was animated, and he had lifted himself up in his chair with his arms.

"Father! Be calm."

"Never mind calm. We must get that young man out of that place. He shall come here."

"Here, father? How can we do that?"

"Tomorrow we will get that doctor in. He must know someone who can make crutches for me."

"I'm sure he will know someone, but is it not too soon? And what are you intending to do?"

"As soon as I can move, I will visit the First Consul. He visited my house in Brittany, and we know where that led, and he can hardly turn me down. That young man is a prisoner of war, and should be treated as such. Damn Fouché's games. He can kiss my arse."

Odile and Dominique looked at each other and smiled at Morlaix's sudden energy. Perhaps there was hope, for him and for Jack.

Although, since Dominique's visits had started, and I suspected the distribution of silver, the guards had become very much more respectful, the pair who came to my room that morning were not communicative.

"Come with us."

I felt a shiver of fear. "Where are you taking me?"

"Never you mind. Come along."

Down the long flights of stairs we went and entered the governor's room.

He rose from his table. "Midshipman Stone. A carriage awaits you outside. It has been a pleasure to have you as our guest."

As far as I could tell, he spoke without irony.

"A carriage? Where am I being taken?"

He did not answer, but gestured to the guards, who took me outside and bundled me into a public carriage. They sat beside me as we made our way through the streets of Paris, lively and noisy. I did not understand what was happening. Was there to be a trial? The carriage stopped, one of the guards got out and knocked on a high, shiny door, and to my astonishment I realised where I was. I had been there before. Morlaix's house!

The door opened, and Dominique and another woman, who I guessed must be her mother, came towards the carriage, accompanied by a burly servant. Dominique embraced me and then turned towards Madame Morlaix. "Jack, this is my mother."

I was struck dumb, and could hardly control my emotions. I had thought that I was being taken to some tribunal, to be tried for an offence against the French state, and here I was, not in a court, but inside the house which I remembered as though from a faintly remembered dream, opulent, with delicate, exquisitely carved furniture. All I could do was nod, but Madame Morlaix embraced me.

"Jack, you are welcome."

I heard myself speak, in a small voice, in English. "Thank you, Mrs Morlaix."

Dominique laughed, and her mother smiled. "We prefer French in this house, Monsieur Stone, or at least Breton!"

"Yes, Madame Morlaix, it shall be French as I know no Breton."

They took me upstairs to a bedroom, huge and airy with high windows, and sat me on a chair. On the floor was a shining copper bath. As I watched, a maid came in and poured a jug of steaming water into the bath, and returned shortly with another.

"Jack," said Madame Morlaix, "you should take a bath. We have put some of my husband's clothes out for you in the closet there. They will not be a good fit, but nevertheless …."

I managed to stay awake in the bath, then dressed myself, and sat on the bed. There was a knock on the door, and Madame Morlaix came in. I went to stand up, but I was rather slow about it, and she motioned for me to stay on the bed.

"How are you, Jack?"

"I am much better already, but I do not understand why I am here. How long am I to stay? What about the charges against me?"

"You are here, Jack, because of Dominique's affection for you and my husband's influence. He petitioned the First Consul, who ordered that you were to be released into our care, at least until you have recovered. Napoléon believes that you should be treated as a prisoner of war."

Napoléon had ordered my release! I had not until that moment had much regard for Bonaparte, but I felt a shift in my perception of him. I started a slightly incoherent speech of thanks, but Madame Morlaix, always one for practicalities, or "modalities" as she called them, held up her hand and stopped me.

"Jack," – she actually said "Jacques" in the French manner, and from that time onwards I have always been Jacques – "are you well enough to take something to eat?"

"Yes, thank you," was all I could say, and suddenly I found I was ready for lunch.

Morlaix's interview with Bonaparte had gone well. The First Consul was contrite, or at least pretended to be, which surprised and disarmed Morlaix.

After they had exchanged pleasantries, Bonaparte declared, "Breton, what can I say? I was mistaken. I sacrificed a great deal, including your leg, and all your work, for no gain. It seems that what the Spanish used to call the 'Enterprise of England' is undone."

Morlaix heard himself say "I am sorry for that."

Morlaix, with one leg, feeling sorry for Bonaparte? He felt himself to be an imbecile, and that Bonaparte was a sorcerer.

"I understand that you believe I can help you."

"That is my belief, yes, but it is a delicate matter. You will remember my daughter, Dominique?"

"Indeed I do. She was in Brittany with you."

"There is an English Midshipman …."

----------***----------

The visit to Bonaparte had tired Morlaix to the point of exhaustion, and two days later, he was sitting in his chair when Dominique came into his room.

"Father, how are you?"

"I suppose that I am as well as can be expected."

"It is time for lunch. Would you like to sit at the table? We have a guest."

He smiled at her, fleetingly. "A guest? Oh, of course, your Englishman."

"Yes, father, he is here, very weak."

"Very well, I suppose that I have to meet him sometime."

She helped him to a seat at the head of the table. He felt awkward, being helped by his daughter. He sat sideways, his stump on a stool.

There was a knock at the door and Madame Morlaix came in, with Jack following, looking very anxious.

"My dear, this is Jacques, Midshipman Stone."

"I am pleased to meet you, Captain Morlaix."

Morlaix laughed.

"What is it, father?"

"An English officer, in my house, and not only that, wearing my clothes."

"I am sorry, father, that is all we had. And his own …."

"Never mind my dear. Please sit, Jacques."

Morlaix watched, fascinated, as his wife helped the young man to his seat, so frail and anxious-looking in clothes that were far too big for him. The Englishman sat still, looking at his plate.

"Jacques," said Madame Morlaix, "I believe that you have been to this house before."

"Yes, Madame, I have, in happier times, times of peace."

"Did you meet my husband then?"

"No, I did not have that pleasure."

The meal passed well enough. Morlaix felt himself increasingly interested in Jack, and managed to hold him in conversation, asking about his seafaring career.

After the meal, Jack and Morlaix sat together in easy chairs.

"Well, Jacques, we may not have met before, but I think that you have had a considerable effect on me, nonetheless."

"I am afraid that I have, sir, and I believe that I should tell you that we have in fact met before – twice, though not to speak."

Morlaix was dumbfounded. "Twice you say? How was that?"

"Yes, sir. Once in Weymouth, and once in London, at Wapping."

Morlaix thought hard, and had a dim remembrance of a certain vibration in the rigging of a long-departed ship.

"Of course, aboard *Cicely*."

"I was there, sir, and I had seen you in Weymouth, before that."

"My God, had you?"

"Yes, sir, briefly. And, sir, we were only a few feet away when you were at the helm of *Cicely*, and *Waterwitch* spoke us."

Morlaix shouted, energised, and a servant appeared. "Some brandy, please. Midshipman Stone, you must tell me this story."

The brandy arrived, but Jack did not speak. Morlaix could see that he was hesitant.

"Captain Morlaix, I should not have said what I did, and I do not think I should speak further of it."

Morlaix suddenly realised the reason for Jack's hesitation. It was because he had been imprisoned for what he had done, as a civilian, and Morlaix, who was obviously a significant figure in France, had asked him for what amounted to a confession.

"I think I understand your hesitation, Jacques, but I can assure you that I know of your boat-stealing activities, and whatever you say will go no further than between ourselves. You have my word on that."

"The servants, sir?"

"There are none nearby, and if you prefer, we shall speak in English."

"Very well, sir, I will tell you. I did worse than steal a boat, much worse. Do you remember the Mate of the *Cicely*?"

Morlaix did, very well. "Of course, a truly horrible man. A drunkard and traitor, but I made use of him. He into the sea at Carteret, drunk, and I don't believe he was missed." Realisation suddenly came to Morlaix. "Oh, I see …."

"It was me. It was terrible, but it was him or me, and I still feel I had no choice."

"It was a war, Jacques, terrible things happen in war, and even worse things in revolutions, when ordinary men and women can become monsters. Please tell me, it will go no further."

"Well, sir, my father is a fisherman."

Morlaix smiled. "So was mine, in Rosko."

"Mine is in Portland, we were nearly caught by the Revenue, so he apprenticed me to Captain Wellstead, of the *Cicely*. He wanted me away from the smuggling."

"In Rosko, smuggling is a big business, or was before the blockade."

"Well, I was off watch when you boarded us …."

Morlaix sat back in his chair and listened.

Chapter 40 – Convalescence

To Odile's intense relief, dinner that evening was, Odile thought, the most cheerful meal they had had for a long time. The two men were gravely wounded, it was true, but they seemed happy, relieved, Odile thought, that for the time being they were safe, they had made their contribution, and at least, for a time, the war could get on without them.

Dominique looked happier, thought Odile, than she had been since the night of the party at their house when she had first met Jacques. The strain of caring for him and her father had been very great, Odile knew, and Jacque's incarceration in the Temple had been almost more than she could bear.

But now they were here, round the table.

"Odile," said her husband, "did you know that Jacques' father was a fisherman, like mine?"

"I doubt if your father," said Odile "ever set a net in his life. The rum came into Roscoff, and he took it out again, Guernsey or even to England. He lived rather well, didn't he, for a fisherman?"

Her husband laughed. "True enough. I believe Jacques' father was also a firm believer in free trade."

Odile saw Jack glance at Odile, and a small smile pass between them.

"He was, sir, a firm believer."

----------✳✳✳---------

The weeks passed, and the invalids grew stronger with each day. Morlaix and Jack frequently went together to the library, Jack helping Morlaix down the stairs.

Odile even had a small "at home", which went very successfully, though they were careful to keep Jack out of the way and did not speak of him. Odile knew that the bond between Jack and Dominque was deep, and growing, and it was no surprise when, one morning when they were drinking what was purported to be tea (the effects of the Royal Navy's blockade meaning that colonial goods were scarce) in the drawing room, Dominique said, "Mother, you must know that I would like to marry Jacques."

That evening, Odile broached the subject with her husband.

"He is a fine young man," he said "very fine, but I do not know what his future is. He appears to have no desire to return to his naval duties, and has a great horror of war. And anyway, as things stand, with Fouché and the criminal accusations, it will be difficult to exchange him as a prisoner of war. His interests seem to be in machinery, steamboats and the like. As you know, he was an avid pupil of Fulton. With the nations at war, I do not see that he could become a Frenchman without feeling that he had betrayed England."

Odile glanced at her husband: "He is not the only one tired of war. I think that all of us in this house wish to have nothing more to do with it. I have been considering what could be done. There are difficulties, but I have the outline of a plan. Listen …."

Later that week, as dinner was finished, Odile looked at her husband, who nodded.

"Jacques, Odile and I have something to discuss with you."

The mood instantly became serious, Jack's expression in particular becoming one of deep concern.

"We know that you wish to marry."

Jack's face became red with embarrassment, and he stammered, "I know that I am young, but I am not entirely penniless. I have a pension from the …."

He became even more embarrassed at the thought of making such an admission in a republican household.

"Never mind that. In normal circumstances I would urge you to wait, you are both young, and the times are uncertain, and, Jacques, I wish to make plain that you are very welcome in our house. However, you are not entirely secure here, and it is possible that Fouché's star may rise higher again. We have considered whether you could become a citizen of the Republic."

"I could not do that, sir, not with the war."

"Well said, Jacques, you are quite right," agreed Morlaix, "but we have an alternative scheme. We have spoken of it to Dominique, and she is in favour of it. Listen and I will explain."

I had sat with Dominique on the small sofa in the room on the first floor, which looked out over the street, for what seemed like hours. And now, as I lay in my bed, my soft, luxurious bed, I thought about what we had discussed. Her parents' plan, well, the Morlaix family's plan, was that Dominique and I should marry, and we should take ship to America, where Madame Morlaix's sister was established, and who would, it was hoped, be able to help me find work in some field with good prospects. Captain Morlaix, of course, had spent considerable time in America, and was enthusiastic about the place.

It was to be admitted that there were several difficulties involved with the plan. Fouché was unlikely to be pleased that I had escaped from his clutches, I was a serving member of the British Navy, and by no means least, that same Navy was blockading France. If I was caught, well, it did not bear thinking about.

I had come to hate war, it was true, and had intended to resign from the Navy as soon as I returned to England, but that was a very different matter from a serving officer escaping to America when the nation was at war.

In the morning, after a sleepless night, I went to see Captain Morlaix. By then, he was moving well on his crutches, and was becoming quite cheerful.

"Sir, I would like to have your advice."

"Of course, Jacques," he smiled, calling me by a name I was becoming very used to.

"I expect the rules of the French and English navies are similar, are they not?"

"I am not sure that they are exactly the same, but I believe that they are not likely to be very different. Are you worried that you would be acting badly if you were to leave for America?"

"Yes, sir, I am. It is not only the legal position, but I believe that England is engaged in a just war against Bonaparte. We are defending ourselves."

"Well, Jacques, I cannot really say about that. We would say that we are protecting our revolution."

"I know, sir. And the Navy, well, it has given me a chance that I would not otherwise have had."

"I am sure you would have done well at sea in any event."

"Thank you, sir, but I do not know what I should do."

"You should resign, Jacques, and leave France. If Fouché loses interest in you, something he is not known for, you will be a prisoner of war, and eventually you will be exchanged, and you will be back in the British Navy. You will not see Dominique until the war is over, and I have to say, Jacques, that I do not think that peace is very close."

"I know, sir."

"I am Dominique's father, and I want the best for her. Of course, if she goes to America it will be sad to part from her, but the alternative, losing you, will affect her greatly. You are young, but you have made a great contribution to your country, more than most men make in their lives. You have no reason to feel that you are doing anything wrong."

"If I resign from the Navy, sir, how could I do it?"

"In the French Navy, one has to write a letter, and wait for a reply. I am sure the same applies in your Navy. I believe that your letter should lay stress on your injury as the main reason for your resignation."

"If I write such a letter, how can it be sent to England?"

"Think about it, Jacques, you know very well!"

"Oh, I see, sir, you mean by, by the free trade."

That evening I wrote the letter and gave it to Captain Morlaix.

Afterwards, I remembered the next two weeks in that beautiful house as a fantastic dream of happiness, although there was an underlying sense of tension, because of the possibility that Fouché could interrupt the dream. We had an advantage because we did not have to leave the house to marry, as the revolution meant that weddings did not have to take place in church, and clergymen no longer officiated.

Dominique and I spent a long time with her parents, planning our journey, and what we would do when we arrived in America. It seemed that Madame Morlaix's sister was well established in the state of Delaware, and it was proposed that we should travel there when we arrived. As I have discovered in later life, matters such as this are always made simpler when money and influence are available, and the Morlaix family had both.

Dominique and I were married on a bright autumn morning, the sun shining through the tall windows of the library. A clerk from the Ministry of Marine, known to Captain Morlaix, officiated. Morlaix's former coxswain, Paul Kerjean, was one witness, and the housekeeper from Brittany, Peress, the other. After a meal with Dominique's parents, which was charged with extreme emotion, and at which little food was consumed, I said my goodbyes.

Madame Morlaix embraced me, her face wet with tears. "You are a good man, Jacques, I am sure that you will look after my daughter."

Captain Morlaix leaned his crutch on the table. "Jacques, since you have been in our house, you have become my friend, and now you are my son. I should tell you before you leave that, as soon as I can be excused from my duties to the Republic, Odile and I likewise intend to travel to America. We have no family here, and I am not inclined to resume my naval career."

I left the house through a rear door, dressed in the old clothes that had been bought for me in the last few weeks. It was many weeks since I had been out of the house, and it was a strange experience to walk the few hundred yards to an alley where Kerjean, a small wiry seaman, was leaning against a wall.

He looked at me and smiled. "Bonjour, Jacques Pierre."

It had been agreed that I would completely Frenchify my name, and, if asked, in France, claim to be an American seaman of French descent. Jacques Pierre was the name that appeared on my marriage certificate. Captain Morlaix would undoubtedly eventually be challenged about my absence, but he and Madame Morlaix intended to make no excuse for my escape, but rather rely on their connections with Bonaparte and Talleyrand to smooth over what they hoped would be considered a rather trivial matter, citing the fact that I was now their son in law, and that they were protecting me from the poor treatment that Fouché had already subjected me to.

We set out through the streets of Paris in a northerly direction, hoping that if Fouché's men noticed my departure from the house, they would assume that I meant to travel to the Channel coast and from there make my escape to England.

It was a very anxious time, but there appeared to be no sign that we were followed, and eventually we circled back and headed south, crossing the Seine near the famous cathedral. We passed through the *porte* without difficulty, and, at the coaching inn, sat down to wait. After two hours or so of insufferable tension, at least for me, we were joined by Dominique, who had been escorted by Peress. We were reunited with our baggage, two small chests, and within the hour were travelling towards the south in a rather crowded diligence, a big four-wheeled coach pulled by a large team of horses.

Our honeymoon was spent on the journey south, a cheerful time when it became clear that we were not being followed. Dominique was very happy, most of the time, although sometimes she was made sad at the thought of leaving her parents and France. But she was young and adventurous, and the lapses into melancholy were brief. In short, we had a wonderful time. The diligences were rather slow and often uncomfortably full, but the system was well organised. The coaching inns were of variable quality, but I think we hardly noticed.

After several days, we alighted with our luggage, and watched the diligence continue south, to Bordeaux. Captain Morlaix's intelligence was that we might find a ship for America at Pauillac, on the left bank of the Gironde, and that the small port of Pauillac would be safer for us than waiting for a ship in the large city of Bordeaux, as news of our departure from Paris might reach Fouché's men there.

We were set down by a carrier at an inn in the town of Blaye, on the opposite side of the Gironde from Pauillac, where we were assured there was a ferry across the estuary. Enquiries at the inn revealed that the ferry would not depart until the following morning, so before dinner we decided to walk down to the estuary to see the place where the ferry ran from. We were rather surprised to find that Blaye was a larger place than we had imagined, and dominated by an enormous stone fort. The fort seemed to be at a high state of alert, with a considerable number of soldiers on the ramparts. The estuary was so large that we could only just make out the opposite bank.

We heard a gun fire from the fort, and then another, and the acrid smell of powder drifted across us as smoke. Suddenly, a ship hove into view from behind the fort, moving slowly upstream against the swift-flowing, muddy tide, perhaps two cables off. With a sinking feeling I saw the huge ensign at her peak, and knew her for a British frigate.

"Probably *Pallas*," I said to Dominique. "She was briefly in Guernsey when I was there. She's new."

We watched the frigate, smart and resplendent in black and yellow, fire her broadside, slowly, deliberately at the fort, one gun at a time, each report accompanied by cheering from the crew. The soldiers on the ramparts disappeared, keeping their heads down, and we heard the balls scream across the water and the noise as they smashed into the fort.

The ship tacked, smartly, and suddenly the tide was with her, and she disappeared towards the sea. The raid must have been timed to the minute. We walked back to the inn, through an excited crowd.

"What did you think, Jacques, when you saw the ship?"

I considered her question. "Pride, I think. I may be Jacques, but I am still an Englishman."

"I thought, all my life I have been the daughter of a naval man, and now I have married one. I have spent much time on warships, but that is the first time I have seen a warship in action, and watched what you seamen do."

"A solitary frigate, bombarding a fort, twelve leagues from the sea. Most seamen don't do that. Cochrane does though."

"Lord Cochrane? I believe my father has often spoken of him."

"I'm sure he has. He is famous in our Navy, and no doubt in the French one as well. He's well known to the public in England."   I paused a moment, thinking. "I must say, Dom, seeing that smart ship, so beautifully handled, almost in the middle of France, may have made me proud as a British sailor, but it did not make me wish I was aboard, playing my part. I really have had enough of that."

"I am very glad, Jacques. Let us try and forget war."

Next morning, early, we breakfasted at the inn. I kept my own counsel as the proprietor engaged Dominique in conversation, recounting an undoubtedly exaggerated account of the actions of *Pallas*. It seemed that the French public as well as the English was well acquainted with her and her commander.

"Her captain, Lord Cochrane, they call him 'Sea Wolf'. He has almost stopped the trade from Bordeaux, and yesterday drove a fine French warship aground before he came here. There are many complaints from the citizens about our Navy."

We made our way through the town to the ferry, and before long were sailing across the muddy water – or watery mud – of the Gironde. There was no sign of *Pallas* or the "Sea Wolf", and I assumed they had made their way to their station at the mouth of the estuary, to resume the blockade.

At Lamarque, on the left bank of the Gironde, we hired a cart pulled by a solitary horse, and before long were in Pauillac, a small port set amongst vineyards. Captain Morlaix had given the address and a letter of introduction to a former shipmate of his who had retired there as a ship chandler. As we got near the port, with a start of something like exultation, I saw a rakish-looking ship alongside a pier, flying a large American ensign.

"Look, Dominique, the Stars and Stripes. Perhaps we are in luck."

She smiled at me. "Perhaps we are."

Dominique knocked on the door of the house whose address we had been given. The door was opened by a woman.

"Bonjour, Madame. Monsieur Darraq? We have a letter for him."

The woman nodded, and beckoned us into a large room which was hung with all sorts of ship's gear, and had a familiar tarry smell. At a bar in the corner, under a grey cloud of tobacco smoke, several men sat on high stools, who I was sure were ship masters. They looked round at us enquiringly, and then returned to their conversation.

The woman spoke to the man behind the bar, and he came over to us.

"In private, please," said Dominique to the man.

"Of course." He led us to a side parlour.

"Monsieur Darraq?"

"Yes, mademoiselle."

"I believe you know my father, Captain Morlaix."

"Indeed I do, Mademoiselle."

"I have a letter from him." She handed him the letter, which he read.

He let out a long breath. "I think you had better come upstairs, Madame and Monsieur."

We went upstairs to Darraq's living quarters.

"I served with your father for a long time, Madame. In the Midi. Is he well?"

"Unfortunately he was wounded, at St Malo. He has lost a leg, but is recovering."

"I am very sorry to hear that. I was with him when he was wounded before – his head. When he is recovered perhaps he will come here and chase off that damned Cochrane. The Navy here…" He shook his head. "Yesterday a sloop ran herself aground rather than engage him. You have need of a passage, to America?"

"We do," said Dominique. "We saw an American ship in the port."

"There is one there, *Payoff*, Captain Molineux, from Baltimore. They call her a clipper, very fast. She has been loading wine, and her cargo has been complete for two weeks. But Cochrane …," he continued, "Cochrane may not take an American ship, even though he is enforcing the blockade, because it might cause an incident with the United States, but he is playing games with her crew. Last week he appeared just after dawn, and backed his topsails a few yards off the jetty. Our guns were not ready, of course, but *Pallas* was stopped only a few feet from *Payoff*. He asked if there were any volunteers for the English Navy! There were not, of course, but the men were very worried, as the English Navy considers Americans to be British, and liable to be pressed into service if their ship is boarded. Some of *Payoff*'s crew have deserted and gone to Bordeaux."

We heard this news with rising alarm, and for the first time I realised what it was like to be on the wrong side of the Royal Navy's blockade of France.

"You must stay here, with us, while we decide what to do. This afternoon, I will ask Captain Molineux to visit you."

Dominique felt as though her future was slipping away, largely through the actions of Lord Cochrane and his *Pallas*. As they had travelled south, and the possibility of pursuit by Fouché's agents had receded, she had gradually felt happier. Yesterday, when she had seen the Gironde for the first time, she had really believed that they could escape. And then, the ship, *Pallas*, beautiful in the late evening sunshine, firing on the fort, and interfering with their plans. If her father was here, she thought, the damned ship would probably be alongside a quay in Bordeaux, flying a tricoleur. And there was an American ship here, a strange-looking thing, but nevertheless a ship that could take them to America, if only it wasn't for Cochrane and his frigate.

At about six o'clock, Darraq came into the room, accompanied by a tall thin man, who bowed.

"Molineux, Madame and Monsieur, master of the *Payoff*, moored yonder."

He spoke in English, and Dominique looked at Jack, as her English was still imperfect. She had not yet used it to speak to anyone except Jack.

Jack answered, "Captain Molineux, I am Jacques Pierre, and this is my wife, Dominique. We require a passage to the United States, and we would go in your ship, if you have room for us."

Dominique could tell that Jack was exaggerating his French accent.

"I have room for you, sir and madam, good quarters, too, and a fast passage guaranteed, but that damned frigate has frightened some of my crew, who have cleared off to throw themselves on the mercy of the American consul at Bordeaux, God help them."

"Is your ship loaded, Captain?"

"She is, sir, these last three weeks. Finest Bordeaux wine. It'll find a ready market and a good price in Baltimore, if I can get it there."

"Captain, we are willing to pay for our passage now, and take our chance that you will be able to take us."

"Very well, Monsieur Pierre."

After Dominique had paid the requested amount, Molineux departed, and she and Jack were left to their own devices in Darraq's house. Several days passed with no change, and

Dominique felt the tension rise in her and her husband. From the window of their room, which they hardly left, they could see the American ship at the jetty, loaded deep, pulling at her mooring lines in the strong tides of the Gironde, as though impatient to depart.

One evening, they heard the door to the chandlery slam, followed by an exited buzz of conversation, and watched as a man left the chandlery, hurried across the street in the driving rain, and boarded the American ship. A few minutes later the man returned in the company of Captain Molineux. The pair went into the chandlery.

"News, I think," said Jack, and Dominique's heart pounded in her chest. "I will go to the chandlery, and ask what is happening."

Dominique put her hand on the door handle, just as Molineux burst through and started to speak excitedly.

"News from Pointe de Grave, at the end of the estuary. The French have men watching from there, and they sent a messenger, who has just arrived. The English ship, *Pallas*, has gone aground, on a shoal off Royan, on a falling tide. She'll be stuck until the next tide floats her. If I had a few more men I'd make the most of this and clear out."

Dominique had understood nearly all of this, but Jack translated for her. As he spoke, an idea came to her, and she spoke directly to Molineux.

"How many men in your crew?"

"I had fourteen, and now only six are left."

Dominique struggled for the right words. "If you had two more, would it be possible?"

Jack looked at her in surprise. "What are you thinking, Dominque?"

"You and I, Jacques, we can help work the ship."

"Dominique, I can certainly work the ship, but you?"

"Don't be a fool, Jacques. I am my father's daughter, and I have spent a long time with him on ships and boats. I can pull on a rope and steer."

Jack thought, and spoke to Molineux. "Captain, Molineux. We have a suggestion. I am a seaman, and my wife" – Dominique had still not become used to being spoken of as a "wife" – "is the daughter of a naval captain, and has experience of handling boats …."

Dominique listened, understanding nearly all of the exchange, and watched the captain's face as its expression changed from one of uncertainty to what seemed to be determination. Outside, the wind lashed the rain against the building.

Jack turned to Dominique. "He says we will go, as soon as we can. The ship is ready for sea. We will have the tide under us for an hour or so, and we should be at Cardouan about dawn. The weather is not pleasant, but Molineux's family is from here, he says he 'knows the road', and believes he can get the ship out of the estuary and into the Bay of Biscay."

He looked at her. "Dominique, the mouth of the Gironde is very dangerous in weather like this, even with Molineux's local knowledge. It will be quite perilous, even without *Pallas*. And afterwards, if we get out to sea, the work will be very hard."

She felt a wave of affection for Jack. "We must try. If we do not, someone will betray us, and you may end up back in the Temple." She saw that Jack was going to object. "I could not bear it if that happened. We will go. I am a republican, and I say 'damn your Lord Cochrane'."

"Very well." Jacques turned to Molineux and nodded. "We will be aboard directly, Captain."

They made frantic preparations for departure, packed hurriedly, and said their goodbyes to Madame Darraq, handing over a letter to be sent to Dominique's father, written in the vaguest terms, but which they hoped would communicate their intentions. With the help of Darraq, they heaved their trunks aboard a trolley, and walked across the windswept street. As they went along the jetty, Dominique felt her confidence begin to slip. The weather was so bad that gusts of wind blew them off their course, and it was almost dark.

"She's what they call a clipper, Dominique," said Jacques, seeing her unease and attempting to distract her. "Topsail schooner, very fast, though I doubt we'll be carrying much sail tonight."

Molineux met them as they went aboard. "I'll show you where to put your dunnage." He looked at Dominique, or, more exactly, at the clothes she wore (formerly Jack's, but now with a dash of emergency tailoring). "I see you mean business, ma'am."

Molineux showed them their quarters, and left. When they returned to the deck, there was a bustle of activity, though the crew seemed very sparse for a ship with such enormous spars.

"Can you take the helm, ma'am?" asked Molineux. "It is the lightest work in the ship, and I believe I would be better employed in pulley hauling with the men."

"I believe I can, Captain."

Jack looked at her, smiling. "I think you mean 'Aye, sir'!"

Dominique went to the wheel with Jack. It was almost as high as she was, and there was a small grated platform for the helmsman to stand on. The binnacle lamp gleamed softly, and she could clearly make out the white compass card. Together, they gave the wheel an experimental turn.

"Pretty light," said Jack, "though it will get heavier when she's moving. See the Turk's head knot on this spoke here? That's so you can feel where the wheel is. You can drop these loops over the spoke to hold the helm. Now, wind her hard over to port."

Dominique wound the wheel until she felt it come up against a stop.

"And now hard a starboard," said Jack. Dominique turned the wheel in the opposite direction. Jack, who had been counting said. "Six turns hard over to hard over, so three from hard over to midships."

Captain Molineux joined them, and Jack conferred with him.

"Dom, I just checked what the helm orders are; there's sometimes confusion about which way to turn the wheel. When he says 'port wheel' you are to turn the helm this way ..."

Dominique listened as Jack explained the system on the American ship, which, despite the situation, rather irritated her, as it was exactly the same as was used on French ships, and, she thought, probably English ones as well.

"We are ready, then. Jacques, with me please," said Molineux.

"Aye, sir."

They went forward, leaving Dominique at the wheel, softly illuminated by the binnacle lamp. She heard orders given, and dimly saw the inner fore staysail climb up its stay, and heard it flogging in the wind. She heard Molineux shout, "Hard a starboard."

"Aye, sir, hard a starboard." She turned the wheel, and felt the ship respond to the tide rushing over the rudder. From the bow of the ship, she heard men curse as they strained against the capstan bars, and then, after what seemed a long time, the clink of the capstan pawls as the cable came in. Jack ran past her, shouted to a man ashore, and pulled a dripping mooring rope aboard. He ran back forward, waving to Dominique as he passed. The clink of the pawl came faster, and the gap between the jetty and the ship widened.

She heard a shout, "Up and down," and then men tramping along the deck, sheeting in the staysail.

"Midships," called the captain, and she acknowledged the order, and turned the wheel. The ship was moving now, she could feel the wheel vibrating in her hands.

"As she goes," came the order from forward, and suddenly Jack was at her side.

"Keep the wind just there," he said. "Watch the staysail, we're going to get the mainsail on her."

Dominique concentrated hard, feeling the wind on her face, and keeping the ship pointed so that the staysail just started to flap. Men climbed along the huge boom above her head, reefing the mainsail, and then she could see them working round the mainmast, hoisting the great sail, which rose very slowly, the gaff swinging in the wind. Too few men, thought Dominique, as she spun the wheel, struggling to keep the slowly moving ship's head into the gale. At last the sail was hoisted, and the men paused briefly, recovering, before moving to the mainsheet and sheeting the sail home. The ship heeled and gathered way, and Molineux joined her at the wheel.

"How is she?"

"Answering well, sir."

"Put the helm up and lay her off eight points, course about north. I will watch for the gybe. You men there, at the mainsheet."

As the ship turned away from the wind, she started to move quickly, the few lights on the shore sliding past.

Dominique was relieved at the helm by one of the sailors, an American.

"Good evening to you, miss," he said as he took the wheel. "Jackson is the name, bosun, from Baltimore. We do not have many women ABs. Have you been long at sea?"

"Not long, Jackson, indeed this is my first trip."

"You certainly have picked a nice night for it."

The ship rushed on, the low bank of the estuary barely seen in the dark. Judged by the occasional shore light, she was making good progress towards the sea, even against the tide as it turned and began to flood into the Gironde.

Later, Molineux grew concerned that they would arrive at the entrance while it was still light, and with Dominique at the helm again, the crew went through the exhausting exercise of handing the mainsail to slow the ship, continuing under the staysail alone. The sky cleared, and the wind backed to the north.

Gradually, the sky became lighter in the east, revealing a bleak scene, the muddy water almost covered in froth from short, breaking waves. Dominique shivered in the cold, keeping her eyes on Jack, who was high in the foremast rigging, sent there as he was the youngest aboard and therefore assumed to have the best eyesight.

"On deck there! I can see a frigate. Point on the starboard bow." He pointed his arm, and slid rapidly down the rigging to the deck, and ran aft to speak to Molineux.

"Pretty sure its *Pallas*, sir, about a league distant. She's on an even keel. I don't know if she's still aground or anchored."

"We've left it rather late, I believe," said Molineux, and shouted, "All hands."

"We must shake the reefs out out the mainsail."

This was a laborious process with the lack of crew, but when they sheeted in the enormous sail, the ship started to fly through the choppy water, heeling so that water crashed over the lee bulwarks and sluiced along the decks. Dominique watched as a huge American ensign was hoisted at the main peak.

"Old Glory," said Molineux to Dominique, "perhaps that'll give 'em pause. She's a cracker, my ship, ain't she?" And then to Jack, "Up on the foretop again, and have a look at that damned frigate."

Dominique felt a stab of concern as she watched Jack climb the steeply sloping foremast.

"On deck there! It's *Pallas*, making sail."

Dominique could see the frigate herself now, not far off. Jack returned from the rigging, and Molineux spoke to him. "Naval man, are you?"

"Former naval man, sir."

"Have you seen much action?"

"I have, sir."

"I've an idea of what to do, but I'd appreciate your views, as a former naval man. Quickly, mind."

"I've been in a frigate chasing a schooner, sir, and the schooner took advantage of tacking more quickly, and sailing closer to the wind. If we come up close to her, and then haul our wind, she'll take a bit of time to come round."

"I believe you're right, Jacques. Miss, help Jackson at the helm, it's mighty heavy with her going like this."

He shouted, "Standby staysail and main sheets." The men moved on the deck.

Dominique, standing with Jackson at the helm, could see every detail of *Pallas*, beautiful in the sunshine as she bore down on the schooner, her guns run out and sails straining in the gale. The distance between the ships closed rapidly, until it seemed that a collision was inevitable, when Molineux shouted, "Helm down. Sheets as she comes up, then put her hard on the wind."

Dominique heaved on the wheel with Jackson, moving it almost one spoke at a time. As the ship turned to starboard, up into the wind, the sails momentarily flogged, allowing the crew to sheet them in. Dominique and Jackson put the helm up, and almost instantly the ship heeled over.

From the corner of her eye, Dominique saw the frigate rush past, turning, but too slowly. A uniformed man on her poop deck shouted through a speaking trumpet, but his words were torn away by the gale.

Twenty minutes later, the schooner was back on course heading for the sea, but the larger frigate had tacked quickly and was not far behind, sailing quickly. The frigate fired a gun, but the range was extreme, and they did not see where the shot went.

The vista now was expansive, the distant shores of the estuary fringed with breaking waves, and the schooner started to rise and fall as she felt the ocean swell. On the port bow, Dominique could see the famous Cordouan lighthouse, huge and grey against a backdrop of breaking waves. She thought that she had never seen a bleaker sight

Dominique listened as Molineux shouted to Jack above the noise of the wind in the rigging.

"She's catching us. If we can get through the channel, and head up close hauled, we might lose her, but she may catch us before that. It's a long channel."

"I believe you're correct, sir, but I don't know what else we can do."

"Local knowledge, Jacques, it is something that your Navy does not have."

Dominique thought of the story of Sausmarez's exploits at St Malo, and was not sure she quite agreed.

"There is a channel, Jacques, south of Cordouan, I do not think his lordship over there will risk his ship in it. It will be unpleasant in this weather, but not impossible. Stand by at the helm and at the sheets."

The men went back to the sheets. Molineux kept his eyes firmly on the northern shore of the estuary, where Dominique could see two towers, quickly coming into line. Just before they did, the captain shouted, "Helm up, ease the sheets."

The schooner came upright, and ran before the wind, heading into what seemed like an impossible expanse of breaking waves. Now the wind was astern, the sails had little steadying influence, and the ship rolled wildly, from time to time dipping the end of the main boom into the sea.

"Standby the mainsheet, in case she gybes. Watch your helm there."

Molineux, his eyes on the beacons astern, gave minute helm orders. Dominique could hardly believe that there was any passage through the rollers, breaking with a continuous roar on the sand. She was in such awe of the sea that when she heard Jack shout, "*Pallas* is wearing, she's giving up," it hardly registered.

"Another mark coming up. Standby helm and sheets," shouted Molineux.

They turned to starboard, the waves breaking with overwhelming force on the bank which seemed only yards away, Cardouan looking on impassively. And, then, with a rush of elation, Dominique realised that the ship was through, was in the Bay of Biscay, the breakers receding behind them. She was rising and falling to a great swell, but there was no menace in the waves now.

The last Dominque saw of France was the great lighthouse, and shortly the ship was running fast, quite alone, on a blue deserted ocean.

"Nothing between us and America now," said Molineux.

Famous last words, thought Dominique.

Historical Notes

While most of the events described in the book are fictitious, I have tried to make them as historically plausible as possible. There are, however, some anomalies, which may have irritated readers; the most glaring ones are that I have brought forward by several years both the completion of the Rance canal and Lord Cochrane's foray into the Gironde in *Pallas*.

About the Author

Paul Weston

Paul Weston was born in Swanage, in England, and lives in rural Dorset with his wife Sally. He went to sea as an engineer apprentice with the BP Tanker Company, and his subsequent seafaring career included spells with European Ferries and P&O. After leaving the sea and graduating from university with a degree in Mechanical Engineering, he worked for the Bermuda Electric Light Company and in the Technical Investigation Department of Lloyds Register of Shipping,

Paul started and ran Weston Antennas for 20 years, designing and manufacturing large satellite earth station antennas in Piddlehinton, Dorset, and installing them around the world. He left the firm following a dispute with the venture capital investors, and now works as a mechanical engineer with Siemens in Poole, designing traffic control equipment. With several inventions and patents to his name, Paul is very interested in innovation, and is presently developing a new system for electric vehicle charging.

Paul has extensive sailing experience, starting with his family's converted "Fifie", True Vine. As a teenager he sailed from New York to Lymington in a home designed and built 26 foot yacht. He has owned several boats, including *Pegasus*, a Stella class 26 footer which he sailed to the Azores and back, and a variety of dinghies. For twenty two years Paul and Sally owned a Mitchell 31 Sea Angler *Mitch*. In 2018 they renovated *Mitch*, which was in a neglected state in the garden, replacing woodwork, engine, gearbox and electronics. With the work complete, they took *Mitch* over the Channel, across the Bay of Biscay, and into the French canals. In 2021 they emerged from the canals into the Mediterranean, and *Mitch* ventured as far as Porquerolles before returning to England via the Rhone and Seine. *Mitch* was sold in 2022, and Paul and Sally now own a 42 foot aluminium lift keel sailing yacht, *Kadash*, in which they have just completed a Mediterranean cruise, and in which they hope to voyage more extensively in future.

Printed in Great Britain
by Amazon

25459427R00116